Shadows in the Dark

Patricia Rogers

Author's Tranquility Press
Atlanta, Georgia

Copyright © 2023 by Pat Rogers.

All rights reserved. No part of this publication may be reproduced, distributed or transmitted in any form or by any means, including photocopying, recording, or other electronic or mechanical methods, without the prior written permission of the publisher, except in the case of brief quotations embodied in critical reviews and certain other noncommercial uses permitted by copyright law. For permission requests, write to the publisher, addressed "Attention: Permissions Coordinator," at the address below.

Pat Rogers /Author's Tranquility Press
3800 Camp Creek Pkwy SW Bldg. 1400-116 #1255
Atlanta, GA 30331, USA
www.authorstranquilitypress.com

Publisher's Note: This is a work of fiction. Names, characters, places, and incidents are a product of the author's imagination. Locales and public names are sometimes used for atmospheric purposes. Any resemblance to actual people, living or dead, or to businesses, companies, events, institutions, or locales is completely coincidental.

Ordering Information:
Quantity sales. Special discounts are available on quantity purchases by corporations, associations, and others. For details, contact the "Special Sales Department" at the address above.

Shadows in the Dark/ Patricia Rogers
Paperback: 978-1-961123-57-1
eBook: 978-1-961123-58-8

Contents

Chapter 1 5
Chapter 2 10
Chapter 3 16
Chapter 4 18
Chapter 5 21
Chapter 6 24
Chapter 7 27
Chapter 8 29
Chapter 9 33
Chapter 10 36
Chapter 11 41
Chapter 12 50
Chapter 13 55
Chapter 14 61
Chapter 15 67
Chapter 16 73
Chapter 17 82
Chapter 18 86
Chapter 19 90
Chapter 20 100
Chapter 21 112
Chapter 22 135
Chapter 23 146

Chapter 1

With Chelsea as his new bride, the memories of his first wife, and unborn baby boy, the memories had begun to fade. He would always have those memories, but the pain of them, had faded.

As Josh and Chelsea got into the car to leave the wedding, everyone waved and shouting their congratulations. He started the car and pulled out on the street, with tin cans rattling along the pavement. They headed for the hotel, at the lake, unloaded their luggage and went to their room.

It was a beautiful room, with a balcony where they could sit and watch the people, at the lake below. Some were swimming or sailing behind boats. Some were just fishing or relaxing.

Josh held Chelsea in his lap and kissed her soft lips. "It's beautiful here," he said as they looked across the lake to where the trees were budding and they could see clusters of beautiful flowers "would you like to rent a boat and go to the other? Chelsea took his face and gave him a long, passionate kiss.

It's a beautiful island and the lake curves around the end of it. I've been there before."

They went to the dock to rent a boat. When they got to the island, it was beautiful. Flowers grew abundantly and birds bang a regular chorus of song. The tip of the island was sandy, with water so clear, you could see fish swimming and shells scattered along under the water. They saw children wading and shouting with glee when they found a shell. An older couple sat under an umbrella, smiling at the fun the children were having. As Josh and Chelsea approached, the parents smiled happily. "They're having a grand old time, aren't they? We come here four or five times a year. These are our grandchildren and we like bringing them so they can play in the water." "We thought you look too young for these to be your grandchildren. We thought you were their parents" Josh said. "Thanks for the compliment," the man said. "I'm Jack and this is Sarah, but there'll come a time when we can't bring them, so it's best to do it now. You should have brought an umbrella, then you could have sat and watched the waves come in. Honey, I'll bet these two are newlyweds, don't you think so?" "Yes," she said. They have that look. "Come and sit with us. This umbrella is plenty big enough for two more." They sat with the older couple and watched the children. "When you have little ones, the older man said, love them and take care of them because, one day, you'll find you're as old as we are."

Josh laughed and thanked the couple for their courtesy. "I guess we'd better get back to our boat. Nice to meet you." They walked casually along, picking up a shell now and then. As they approached their boat, josh saw a short, chubby man running from the direction of their boat. Then, he turned around, came back and said, "Pretty little wife, you got there. Better take care of her. Accidents happen, you know." Then, he took off running again.

They were almost to shore when they heard a bang and water started gushing into the boat. They both knew how to swim, so they grabbed the rope at the head of the boat and towed it to the boat owner. The owner checked the boat and said, "It looks like someone installed a small explosive they could set off from a distance. Do you know someone who might have done it?"

"No, but I've seen a man twice that looked familiar, but I don't know why."

"I'd advise you to go to the police department and report this. It could be harmless or someone could be after you and your wife."

Josh started to pay for the rental, but the owner refused it. "You're not the one responsible for this. My insurance will pay for it. You be careful and report it."

"Should we go to the Sheriff's office?" Chelsea asked. "I think so." Josh said. "The boat owner has insurance on his boat and it may require a report to pay him."

They asked around until they found the Sheriff's office. Josh went to the desk and said, "Sir, we need to make a report about an incident on the lake."

The officer called another man to his desk. "Marty," he said. "These folks need to file a report about something on the lake."

"Right this way, folks. We'll get this taken care of in a jiffy. Have a seat. What happened?"

"Chelsea and I just got married and we came up here to celebrate. We rented a boat so we could go over to the island. We met a nice elderly couple, so we sat and talked with them and watched the kids play. Then we went back toward the boat and there was a short, chubby man running from the direction of it, then he turned and came back and said, 'pretty little wife, you've got there. Better take good care of her. Accidents happen, you know.' Then he ran off again. He seemed so familiar but I can't understand why."

The officer patted his shoulder and said, "don't worry about it. A lot of people see someone they think they know and when they get close enough, the person they thought they knew turns out to be a total stranger."

The officer said, "we have a sketch artist. Do you think you could give us a good sketch and, that way, we could watch for him? Of course, without any kind of evidence, we can do nothing except talk to him, but he might have seen something suspicious."

Josh agreed to do the sketch. He hoped describing the man might help him. When the sketch was done, Josh studied it but still felt as if he had seen the man before but couldn't understand why he felt that way.

As they left the police station, the officer escorted them to the door, congratulated them on their marriage and told them to let them know if there were any more problems.

When they got back to their room, Josh stood staring out the window, trying to figure out why he thought he had seen the man before. Chelsea put her hand on his shoulder and said, "why don't we go out on the deck and relax. It's such a beautiful day and I've really love to sit in my husband's lap and give him lots of kisses."

Josh laughed, scooped her up and carried her to the balcony, where they spent hours celebrating their love. Finally, they decided it was time they got something to eat, so they went to the hotel dining room, where they had a delicious dinner with a glass of champagne. Josh started to take a bite of crab and, when he looked up, he saw the man that had been by the boat. "That's him! He was at the church door and the lake! Why can't I figure out why I know him?"

Chelsea put her arms around his neck and hugged him tight. "Honey," she said, "he's probably staying here, in the hotel and you've seen him. Don't worry. "

He gazed into her emerald green eyes and stroked her flame red hair, "you're right," he said. "He probably is staying in this hotel and I've seen him and just imagine I've seen him before." He lowered his head and laid his lips on the rose pink of hers. The kiss was sweet and rich. As the evening came, they went out on the balcony and watched the beauty of the sunset.

"I wish we could stay here forever, Chelsea said. But we can't leave Maud and Bo anxiously waiting for us."

"I know," Josh said. "We'll get packed and leave in the morning. I'm impatient to see them, too. You and Maud brought me back to life. If I hadn't met everybody at the Bed and Breakfast, I probably would have just kept driving with no place to go. I don't know what I would have done with myself. You were all my saving grace. Falling in love with you was the happiest time of my life."

They sat on the balcony until the moon was full and stars filled the sky with beauty. Then, they went to bed and snuggled together like a pair of puppies. They went to sleep to the sound of music from the beach below.

Chapter 2

On the way back home, Chelsea couldn't help looking at how beautiful things were becoming. The snow was gone, the trees were beginning to bud, and she caught glimpses of flowers peeking through.

"Look how beautiful the flowers are. I didn't realize how much they would have grown by now." Chelsea said. "Look, I can see the front porch. We're almost home."

Josh smiled at her excitement, but he had to admit he was happy to get home, too.

As they walked through the door, they were surrounded by hugs and kisses and "OH 'we're so happy you're back! We've missed you so much. How was the honeymoon? Did you have a good time?"

The questions and answers filled the room. Josh told them about the man he had seen and about what happened on the boat ride. They were all shocked that someone would plant an explosive on the boat. They wondered what kind of evil person would do such a thing.

Josh and Chelsea were tired, so with Bo's help, they unpacked their bags and took them upstairs. They had decided to keep Josh's room because they could look out at the creek and see when the ducks started coming in. Besides, it was a beautiful and comfortable room.

Spring was on the way and as they sat in the recliner, they could catch glimpses of daffodils and the tips of iris coming up. Chelsea sighed and snuggled in close as she watched birds starting to build their nests. Suddenly, she sat up and pointed. "Look, Josh, look. I see a flock of ducks coming toward the creek!"

Josh looked excitedly out the window. "I see them, and, look, and there's another flock coming behind! It won't be long before we can go down and feed them. I wonder how Little Quakers is doing. I think I'll call Frank tonight and see how things are going."

That night, Josh called Frank. "Hello," Frank answered. "Josh, you and Chelsea are back! Sorry I missed the wedding, but the family was with me in China buying a hotel. How did things go?"

"The snow was gone, so Chelsea and I went down to the lake and rented a boat so we could go over to the island. It was beautiful. We met an elderly man and his wife and grandkids. We talked for a while and watched the kids play in the water. Then, we went back to the boat, and we were almost across when we heard a boom and water started gushing into the boat. The boat owner said it looked like someone planted a small explosive that could be set off at a distance."

Frank gasped and said, "why would anyone do something like that? Are you both okay?"

"We're fine, but there was a man I felt like I knew, but I don't know why. It was just my imagination, I guess. The ducks are starting to come, so I called to see how Penny and Quackers are doing."

Frank laughed. "Josh, you wouldn't believe what it's like around here. Every kid in the neighborhood is over here, daily, to play with Penny and Quackers. He follows her everywhere she goes, what she eats he wants, and he snuggles up to her at night."

"We took him with us. We have a little cage he can travel in, and the kids were as excited about him as the kids here. They played games, and one little boy had a small ball he'd roll on the ground, and Quackers would chase it and take it back to Penny. The kids thought it was so funny to see a duck chase a ball, and from the look in his eyes, he was having fun too. Even the adults laughed while watching the kids pay. We all made some good friends there. If I can manage a vacation this year, I think we'll come for a visit. Just take care of yourselves. Bye!"

Josh chuckled and told them about what Frank had said about Penny and Quackers and that they might come for a visit if Frank could manage a vacation in the summer.

"You know Josh said we could take them to see that fancy hotel that was built near town last summer. I hear they have a swimming pool, a golf course and gorgeous suites. I doubt the food is as good as Maud's, but we might check it out."

It was a gorgeous place with beautiful gardens and a large patio where you could just sit and relax. On the top floor, in one of the most luxurious suites, a short, chubby man, dressed luxuriously, sat in a recliner with his feet propped up and an expensive bottle of wine by his side. He was sipping it when a knock came on the door.

"Enter," he said as he took another sip.

The door opened, and two tall, muscular men came in. The tall one was named Bull and had large biceps, shaggy dark brown hair, a squared-off chin, and eyes like black marbles. The other, named Snake, was shorter but massively muscular. His face was scarred as if he had been in several fights. Bull said, "I understand you want us to do a job for you. We already know what it is but want to know when and how much you're paying."

"Pour yourselves a glass of wine and sit by the table. Then we can talk. You know what I want but not how or when."

He stood up and went to a table where he had laid out a small map. "Just up the road is a thick bunch of trees and behind them is a big rock formation. Folks around here call the Climbing Rocks because kids like to climb them and grownups practice rock climbing on them. I want you to climb the back of the rocks and get a good look at the place. Then come back here and tell me about any advantages you see. For just this part, you will each get $200, plus a two-bedroom suite on the second floor of this hotel and access to dining, which I will pay for. In one week, I will tell you to take a look at this picture, he showed them a picture of Josh and Chelsea, and if you see them, you will shoot at them but not hit them. I don't want them dead, yet I want them to start becoming nervous. Once you have shot at them, come back here and relax and enjoy yourselves until I give you the next instruction. You will each receive $400 and all the amenities I named before. But you will shoot at them only when I name the time so that I have an alibi showing I am innocent of any wrongdoing."

The more muscular, shaggy-haired man curled his mouth into a snarl and said, "so you plan to save yourself and leave us blowing in the wind! We know who you are. Your name is Dobie Makil and if the cops catch us, we'll rat on you or just put a bullet in you. You want to pay us chickenfeed while you live the good life."

"Gentlemen, gentlemen, it isn't like that at all. This little vendetta will last three weeks; that last week will be when you kill the man and do what you want with his pretty little wife.

You will then receive $5000 each and transportation from this area. I want them to become increasing afraid, to pay the man for what he did to me. I will leave the day before you kill him, and you will be as safe as a baby in a blanket. I want them so afraid they'll feel like wetting their drawers. Is that more to your liking? If not, I'm sure I can find someone else to do the job."

"We'll go out later on and case the joint. Then, we'll come back and give you the low down. The layout of the place will show us the best way to go about it."

"Good idea. Here's your pay for this week. Let me know what you find out."

They walked out the door, and the tall man turned to the other one. "We're going to keep an eye on that yahoo. I don't trust him. I'm thinking we'll do the job and he'll make sure the cops get us while he alibi's his way out of it. If he double-crosses us, we'll make sure he pays the price for it. Let's go down to those rocks and have a look."

Hands in their pockets, they strolled down the road and ducked into the trees. "Wow." Said the shorter man. "That's some pile of rocks! Shouldn't be too tough to climb, though."

They started the climb but found out it was a little tougher than they thought. Finally, they reached the top and peeked over the edge. There was a field of tall grass that stretched from the rocks to a large building at the top of a small hill. A porch ran from the front entrance and it looked like it ran all the way around the house. On the back were two porch swings and two or three comfortable chairs. Under the porch and around the far end of it was a caged-in area were kennels and several dogs. "I wonder if they use the dogs for police work or run them in the winter," the tall man said.

The other man looked a little nervous. "We better find out. If they're police dogs, they could track us down. I don't want no snarling', barking' dogs after me. I've seen what they can do to a person."

The tall man pointed to the left. "Look over there. I can see a stream and ducks are starting to come in. If we shoot one of them and then, if the guy we're after is in one of the swings or chairs, we shoot at one of the posts, it'll scare them and they'll call the cops, but we'll be gone and they'll think it's somebody practicing for hunting season."

"Yeah, man. You have good ideas. When the cops come to check out the gun shots, we'll be back at the hotel, having a good lunch and a few drinks. They won't have anybody to blame. We'll tell Makil what we found out when we get back and see what he says about the rest of the plan. And we better find out about those dogs."

Chapter 3

After supper was over and the cleanup was done, Josh, Chelsea, and Maud sat out on the back porch and watched the ducks splashing in the stream. Josh was a little nervous about the shots coming so near their heads, but the police had collected the bullets in the post, went down to the Climbing Stones, and collected the casings for analysis. They had come from a rifle, and the officers figured the shots had come from a careless person who was practicing for the fall hunting season. Sometimes hunters were not only careless but highly inept, and that's why they started practicing early. One of the officers told Josh to let them know that if it happened again, they would post a guard to see if they could capture the shooter.

Josh accepted their explanation but still felt there was something strange about the whole thing. At night, he frequently had dreams about a shadowy figure in the dark staring at him. But why have such a dream? He didn't know anyone who might harm him or Chelsea! He started looking out the window into the shadowy darkness in case he could see something strange.

Chelsea began worrying about him because he was so obsessed with the darkness. "Honey," she said. "Everything's going to be all right. The police say it was just someone practicing who wasn't watching what he was doing. Come on. Let's go to bed, and I'll bring you some warm milk to help you sleep."

Josh gathered her in his arms and held her tight. He smiled and then lowered his head to taste her rose-pink lips and he stroked her flame-red hair. "I know, Love, it's just my imagination."

Over the next few days, Josh still dreamed about the shadowy figure, but finally, the dreams faded away, and life got back to normal. He and Bo worked at cleaning up broken branches from the winter storm and touching up siding and shingles that had been blown loose. It took almost a week and a half, but the place soon looked shipshape. Tourists and local folks were coming back to eat, and Maud was happy to see everyone who came in. Since it was April fool's Day, she decided to have a party. She baked a clown cake and had Josh and Bo get a fire going for the outdoor barbeque while she got out wieners and buns and made potato salad. Then, josh went to Anita's and got her and the kids. Meanwhile, Bo went around the neighborhood to make invitations. Stan brought his fiddle, and Josh had his guitar. Soon, the back yard was swarming with people. All the kids and some adults wore masks so they could be April Fools. Two tall masked men came up to Josh, shook his hand, and thanked him for inviting them to the party. He didn't know who they were but was willing to welcome them.

Chapter 4

Soon, there was music playing, dancing, and plenty of laughter. The party lasted until the sun went down and everyone started home. When the two tall masked men left, the shorter one laughed and said, "Well, it was nice of them to invite us to the party. Now, we know exactly what the guy looks like; we're supposed to take it down and that wife of his is a pretty little thing. It'll be a pleasure to have a little fun with her." The other man said, "I think we'll sneak up there tonight and find the best way to get in. Then we'll tell the boss, and he can let us know when he wants it done. But what about the dogs? They'll start barking and snarling?" The tall man said, "I noticed the dogs are kept, in kennels, under the back porch, and around the other side of the building. If we're real quiet, they won't hear us so I'll pick the lock, and we'll go in the door where the party was. Then, we'll find out which room the guy's in. After that, we'll head back to tell the boss." They laughed as they walked back to the hotel.

Josh had been hearing sounds in the night but figured it was just branches still falling from the winter storm, so he snuggled a little closer to Chelsea and went back to sleep. Then, he heard a scratching sound, so he slipped out of bed and down the stairs so he could see out the window in the back door. He watched and shook his head, two raccoons were climbing the back steps and when they reached the top, they climbed into the porch swing and cuddled up together. As he headed back to bed, he couldn't help laughing at the sight of two raccoons cuddling in the swing. Chelsea woke up when he came in the room and asked what he was laughing about. When he told her, she started laughing, too. Then, it was cuddling, laughing, and kissing until they fell asleep again. The next morning, they told Maud and the folks having breakfast about their unexpected fuzzy guests. People laughed and slapped their knees. "You want to be careful having such fuzzy company," one of the truckers said. After breakfast was over and everything was cleaned up, Josh and Chelsea went out on the back porch. Furry hair on the swing was ample proof their unusual guests had spent the night. They cleaned off the swing so any two-legged guests could sit there and not find they were covered with hair. "Do you think they'll come back tonight?" Chelsea asked. "I don't know, but if they do, I'd like to take a picture of them. Just so they don't try to come in the house and cuddle up with us." Josh said with a chuckle.

They went back inside, and Chelsea said, "After lunch and cleanup are done, why don't we go down to the stream and feed the ducks? We haven't been there since they started coming in."

Josh pulled her close and hugged her tight. "I'd like that." He said. "Maybe Maud would like to come with us." They asked Maud, but she just wanted to sit, relax, and do a little crocheting. Little did they know the danger they were in. The two hired killers were peering over the top of the Climbing Rocks, watching as Josh and Chelsea walked down to the stream.

"I wonder how often they go there." The tall one said. "With all those trees, it would be the perfect place for an ambush.

Then we could throw them in the stream, and the cops might think it was an accident. We'll talk it over with the boss and see when he wants it done. I think we'll go down to those trees after dark and scout out a good hiding place." They headed back to the hotel to make their report.

That night, after supper, Stan had decided to stay over and brought his fiddle. "How about a little music?" he said as he took it out of its case. Jose grinned and went to get his guitar. "Anybody else play?" he asked. Chelsea waved her hand and went to the piano in the corner, while Maud went into her bedroom and returned with a harmonica. The men looked slightly astonished because neither knew that the woman played an instrument. Well, it looks like we've got ourselves a band. What do you want to start with? Chelsea thought for a minute and then started with the country. For the next two hours, they jumped from One kind of music to another and finally ended with Gospel. By that time, they were just about worn out.

"You know. Maud said the City Council would be having a charity get-together in the city park. We could supply music, and after we play, I could cook hamburgers and hotdogs."

"Sounds like fun, and I could supply soft drinks," Josh said.

"Don't forget me," Chelsea said. "I know how to make balloon animals we could give to the kids. What do you think? Should we do it?"

"I'm too pooped to pop, and I think I'll hit the sack," Maud said. "And I think we should do it."

Chapter 5

When everyone had gone to bed and the lights were all out, the two killers, wearing black, crept toward the trees and slipped into them. Carrying flashlights, they worked their way through them toward the dock over the stream. On the other side of the dock, the trees were thicker and would provide a better hiding place. The tall man said, "Now, we'll go up to the building and find the best place to get in."

Since the weather was warmer, Bo was letting the dogs out in the fenced area. Their kennels were open if they wanted to be in them, but they had their choice if they were in a playful mood.

As the two men crept, crouched low, toward the building, Rusty's head came up, and he leaped to his feet. A low rumble came from his throat, and he went to the fence. Bella joined him and she began to bark. Soon, more of the dogs joined them, barking and snarling as they watched the approach of the invaders.

Josh heard the noise, rushed down the stairs, and looked out the porch door window. "What's going on?" Bo said as he joined josh. "It looks like two men in black are creeping toward the house," Josh said. They both opened the door and ran to the steps. Bo ran to the dogs and opened their gate. Snarling, snapping and barking, the animals chased after the men. Rusty grabbed one by the leg and shook hard. The man screamed and, tearing free, he headed for the Climbing Rocks Bella tore a piece of the other man's pants leg off, and that man also ran, screaming in terror. Bo whistled the dogs back and locked the gate. "I think we'd better call the Sheriff. Those two were up to no good." I agree. "The short man looked back," Josh said, "and I got a look at his face. I could do a sketch for him." "Go in and get a pair of tongs and a freezer bag and we can put the pants leg in it. That we won't interfere with the evidence. There might even be blood on it that would show DNA." Bo said, "I'll bring some rubber gloves and scissors. Rusty grabbed that one guy's leg, and he might have blood on the hair around his mouth. If so, I'll trim it off and put it in a bag, too. We may have DNA from both guys. I wonder what they were trying to do!" "I don't know, but I want everyone to be careful when they go out." Bo said, "I'm going to put the dogs in their kennels for the night. They need some rest. You know, I think I'll apply for a training class for Rusty and Bella. I think it would be good if the police depart needed tracking or search and rescue dogs available. With all the tourists we have, every year, there's always someone getting lost or hurt in the mountains."

"Especially in the winter." Josh said, "skiers and hikers can be in real danger when the snow is really deep. That's a real good idea. Good luck with it."

They went inside, and Josh called the Sheriff's office. In about ten minutes, a deputy was knocking at the door. It was Deputy Rankin, a man they knew. "I hear you had an attempted break and enter," he said, "what happened?"

"The dogs started barking and growling, Josh said. "I went to look out the window on the back porch and saw two men dressed in black creeping toward the house. Then Bo came down and saw them, so he let the dogs out. Rusty grabbed one by the leg and hung on until the man broke loose. The man screamed and ran, Bella had the other man by the pants leg, but he tore loose, and they both ran toward the Climbing Rocks."

"Did they leave any evidence behind?"

"Yes, there are pieces of pants legs from both of them." Josh answered.

"I hope you didn't handle the samples."

"No, Bo went in and got some tongs and three freezer bags, one for each pant leg, and He brought some rubber gloves and scissors in case Rusty had blood around his mouth hair. He trimmed the hair and put it in the third bag, and I labeled each bag. I've read enough books to know not to mess with possible evidence." He said with a chuckle. "The short man looked back over his shoulder, and I saw his face. If the Sheriff wants his sketch artist to have me come in, just let me know."

"I'll do that. You all need to be careful, especially at night or if you hear sounds. I think the Sheriff will want us to do a drive-by a couple of times during the day and at night. I don't think you'll have more trouble tonight, but I'll do a couple of rive-byes tonight, just in case."

Chapter 6

The men went back to the hotel and pounded on Makil's door. He went to the door and quickly ushered them in. He looked them up and down. "What happened to you?" he asked.

"We were scouting the trees by the stream to find a good spot to take them down. They have canoes, and we were going to strangle them, put them in a canoe, ram it into some rocks and then dump them in the water. The cops would think it was an accident. Then, we started toward the house to see if we could find the best way in. The dogs were out in the penned area, and they started barking and snarling. The guy turned them loose. His lead dog grabbed my leg and liked to rip it off. I finally got loose, but it tore part of my pants leg off. A little dog grabbed Snake's pants, tore a piece out of it, and scrapped his leg. Then we ran with the dog chasings us. Those dogs left evidence of us. We need to find someplace to hide out for a while. We don't plan on getting caught and ending up in jail for what you're paying. Besides, Snake looked back, and they probably saw his face. They might have a sketch made of him."

Makil went into the bathroom and brought out a first aid kit. He handed it to them and said, "Here, clean yourselves up and stay in your room. There's a motel just down the road. Check out here and check into the motel. Dye your hair, get rid of that mustache, and disguise yourselves. Wear different kinds of clothes, and nobody will know it's you. I'll pay for the motel and give you extra for your meals. When you're healed up, call me and I'll tell you what to do. You won't be able to get hold of me for about three weeks because I have some business to take care of. I'll call you when I get back, and we'll take it from there. You've taken on more, so I'll pay $1000 each for the extra. Act like you're just a couple of Joes taking life easy."

Bull and Snake went back to their suite so Bull could take care of the dog bite. Then they checked out and headed for the motel. Makil had arranged for two side-by-side rooms with baths, so they got settled in.

Bull rested his injured leg on a chair and said. "We should shoot those dogs so that they couldn't attack us again. Then, we could take that guy down without any interference!"

Snake shook his head. "If we did that, the cops would really be after us. What we really need to do is hide out in those trees every day until they come down to the creek. They have canoes in that shed, so we could knock them in the head, strangle them, put them in a canoe, ram them into some rocks, and dump them in the water. The cops would think they had an accident."

Bull shifted his leg to a more comfortable position and said. "Sounds good, but I don't like having to hide, in those trees, every day. They might not go down there for days. I can see your point, though. They wouldn't expect anything. Give me a few days for this leg to heal up some and we'll give it a try. Makil will have his alibi since he'll be out of town. Once we've done the Job, we'll call the number he gave us, tell him it's done, find out where he's staying, get our pay, and take off like a scalded cat. If he doesn't come up with the dough, he won't live long. I don't trust him. He seems a little slimy to me."

Snake popped his knuckles and grinned. "I agree," he said. "I think he wants us to take the rap while he gets off, free as a bird. If he double-crosses us, it won't bother me to blow his brains out." He laughed at the idea.

Chapter 7

The following morning, Josh went to the Sheriff's office to do an artist's sketch of the man whose face he had seen. The Sheriff shook his hand and invited him to sit down. "Had you ever seen the men before?"

"No, Sir. They were dressed in dark colors and, coming from the wooded area where the ducks land, hunched over as if they wanted to avoid being seen. Since the weather had been nice, Bo had left the dogs out in the pen. Rusty and Bella saw them and started growling, snarling, and pawing at the fence. Bo came out, and when he saw the men, he opened the gate and let the dogs out. Rusty grabbed the leg of one of the men, and Bella grabbed the pants leg of the other one. Screaming like banshees, the men broke loose and ran for the Climbing Rocks. One was tall and muscular. The other one was shorter and chunky. When he started over the rocks, he turned and looked back. Just as he looked back, the moon came out from behind a cloud and it was very bright. That's when I saw what he looked like. I think he thought the dogs were still after them, but Bo had called them back and gotten them penned up. He's planning to apply for training for Rusty in Tracking and Bella for Search and Rescue. Rusty won the dog pull this year, didn't he? You can't imagine how happy that makes me. We don't have the staff to take care of the local citizens and send out a crew to find someone who's gotten lost or hurt up in the trees or the hills. Tourists come in and think they can hike or camp and never get hurt. We had a man who went on a hike and was supposed to be back before nightfall. It took us two days to find him. He had started down an embankment, and it had been raining, so the ground was soaked, crumbled under him, and trapped under rocks and a tree trunk. We have kids wander off, and we have to find them. You tell Bo if he applies for the training, I'll sponsor him. He could still run his winter business but might save someone's life.

Sheriff Barnes chuckled and, then, led Josh into the room where he could give the sketch artist all the details he had seen. A little later, the Sheriff came into the room and looked at the sketch. "Good job. He said. "We'll send this to several other agencies and see I they have anything on him, and when we get the lab work on the pants legs and blood, we'll let you know if there's any match. In the meantime, be very careful. Lock your doors and stay away from windows. Do you know anyone who has a grudge against you?"

"No, everyone I worked with was a friend. I don't know anyone who would try to harm me or Chelsea or Maud. Maybe they thought we had something valuable they could steal."

"I'll have a copy of this sketch distributed at hotels, motels, and service stations. Maybe we'll find out something that way. Just keep your eyes open." He shook Josh's and patted him on the back. I don't think Maud's guests are in danger because you and Chelsea, Maud, and Bo are the only ones at the house most of the time. Call us if you need us."

Chapter 8

Josh kept a careful watch as he drove home. He told them what Sheriff Barnes had suggested, and they all agreed.

Maud closed the drapes just enough to have light but not enough so their shadows would show. She and Chelsea started moving tables and chairs to safer positions. Any time they went out a door, they checked first. Maud was concerned about her guests, but Sheriff Barnes had said guests were probably safe because they were there for short times, and the danger seemed to come to those who were in the building most of the time, but he still warned them to be careful.

Bull's leg was healing, but he had seen sketches of Snake posted in several places. "Pack all our stuff, he said, we have to get out of here."

"WH-what's going on?"

"When those dogs attacked us, you looked over your shoulder, and that guy saw your face. Now, it's being put up all over the place. I'll go check us out. You go out the back way, but don't let anyone see you. Stay out of sight until I bring the car around. Then, stay out of sight until we're away from the motel."

Snake hurriedly packed all their possessions and then looked up and down the hall and ran to the end and down the stairs. He hid in a dark shadow until Bull came around the back of the building with the car. Bull told him to get in the back seat and stay down until they were on the road. "Where are we going to go?" Snake asked.

"I did a little looking around and saw a deserted building about six or seven miles down the road. It isn't fancy, but we can hide in it. There are plenty of trees to hide the car in when we need to. You stay inside, and I'll drive to a store and get bedding and cots, some deck chairs, a grill, and enough canned food and bottled water to keep us going. In a couple of days, we'll go back and park the car in those trees, by the rocks. Then, we'll go to the spot we thought would be good to hide in. We may have to try it a few times, but when they come to the creek, we'll take them out. We'll get a few days' rest and then try it. Sooner or later, we'll get them. Then we'll tell Makil we're ready for our money."

After a few days of rest and wound healing, they were ready to try. After three days of hiding in the trees near the stream, they saw Josh and Chelsea coming to feed the ducks. Bull motioned Snake in place, and jumped from behind the trees, wrapped a powerful arm around Josh's throat and began to squeeze. Unfortunately for Bull, he didn't realize how strong Josh was and he no longer used a cane but walked with a thick, ornate walking stick and was also very strong. He forced his hand under Bull's arm, ducked his head forward, and, with a powerful swing, brought the walking stick around and slammed it against Bull's head. It hit, with an angle from Bull's jaw and ear. The man screamed and fell backward. When he tried to get up, Josh lashed him across the ribs and kept beating at him until he made it to his feet and staggered toward the Climbing Rocks. Josh took out his cell phone and reported the incident to the Sheriff's office.

In the meantime, Snake pulled out a gun and aimed it at Chelsea. With a sneer, he said, "Too bad. I hate to shoot such a pretty lady, but it has to be done."

Chelsea ducked inside the storage shed and grabbed a canoe paddle.

"Come on out, Pretty Lady. Hiding won't do you any good." Gun aimed, Snake walked in front of the storage shed door, and Chelsea brought the edge of the paddle down, in a savage blow, on Snake's wrist, knocking the gun from his hand. He yelled and grabbed his wrist. Chelsea kicked the gun into the stream and then turned and slammed the flat of the blade across his face, smashing his nose and knocking him head over heels. He scrambled to his feet and ran while Chelsea continued to beat him.

For the first time in their lives, the hired killers found out their victims were more powerful than they were.

Sirens sounded and three police cars pulled into the yard. When Josh and Chelsea told them what had happened and the direction they had escaped in, two squad cars backed out of the yard in time to see the escaping car pull out of the trees and take off. They chased after it but lost it when it went into a large bunch of trees. They had, obviously, planned for possible pursuit. On their way to their hideout, Bull told Snake to pull his cap over his face so no one would recognize him. Then, he pulled into a drive-through and ordered meals for the two of them. Neither felt like fixing something to eat. They were both in too much pain to do anything but lie down. Bull's face and ear were swollen, and he felt like he might have a broken rib or two. Snake's wrist was broken, his nose was smashed, and his body hurt all over.

Sheriff Barnes pulled up to the parking lot and went inside. He gave Maud a hug and said, "Well, what's for lunch today?"

She grinned at him and said, "fried chicken, biscuits and country gravy with apple pie and ice cream for dessert. I suppose you're feeling a little hungry."

He grinned and said, "Maud, you know I'm always hungry for anything you cook. I heard on my radio what had happened and wanted to be sure everyone was okay, and I have some news for Josh and Chelsea. Josh, I sent the sketch nationwide and got real good response and the lab work clinched it. Those two are paid killers. The taller one's name is Bull, and the one in the sketch is called Snake. They're both wanted in six states for murder. One of my officers said they ran because the two of you beat the tar out of them. Good job, but you be careful because they're going to be real mad about what you did, and they'll try even harder to kill you. Josh, do you know how to use a gun?"

"Yes, Sir. I used to enter shooting matches, so I know what I'm doing and my pistol is in Maud's gun locker."

I'd suggest any time you're outside, you have it on. And, Chelsea, I don't know if you can use a gun, but I hear you're real handy with a canoe paddle." He laughed and sat down for a plate of Maud's fried chicken, biscuits, and gravy. A cup of coffee and the pie, with ice cream had him sighing contentedly. As he started to leave, he said, "There will be a squad car patrolling by on a regular basis, and we're going to keep a watch on the trees by the Climbing Rocks. That way, they can't hide a car in those trees. Take care of yourselves and call if you need help."

Chapter 9

Josh had a complete security system installed, in the Bed and Breakfast, with deadlocks and alarms on all the doors and cameras where they could see anyone coming in. The windows also had locks and heavy curtains that could be pulled down at night. The rooms also had locks and a peephole to give customers a feeling of safety.

Josh ensured his weapon was clean and had plenty of ammunition. Since the attacks usually seemed to come from the direction of the Climbing Rocks, he always made sure his body was sheltering Chelsea's. A couple of weeks went by, so they relaxed a bit, but they were still careful.

At night, the dreams Josh had been having for a long time of a dark figure coming toward him started becoming lighter. He still didn't recognize it, but he knew it represented danger. It kept getting lighter until, almost a month later, he sat up, in bed, with a horrified cry, "know who it is!"

Chelsea leaped up and threw her arms around him. "What's the matter, Josh?"

"The man I knew I recognized but didn't know why!" He dropped his face into his hands, "It was the man who caused the wreck that killed my first wife and baby. I remember he was drinking, and he crossed two lanes of traffic and hit our car head-on. It happened so fast; I think that's why it took so long for me to remember. He was put in jail, but I think he was released. Thank God, I finally remembered. It's been haunting me since I came out of the coma. I'm sorry I scared you."

Chelsea hugged him and stroked his hair. "Sheriff Barnes asked if there was anyone who might have a grudge against you. Why don't you tell him about the man? If he's out of jail, he might hold it against you because he had to be put in jail. It wouldn't hurt to tell him."

Josh hugged and kissed her, and they snuggled close together. "You're right. Tomorrow, I'll go to his office and tell him. I'm so glad God put you in my life. He is the rock that has sheltered us from harm, and I know He always will. I know we're going to catch those guys and, maybe, get them to tell us who he is." They cuddled, and Josh smiled as he fell asleep.

The next morning, Josh headed for the Sheriff's office. "Is Sheriff Barnes in?"

The Officer at the desk smiled and said, "He's in a meeting right now, but he should be back in about fifteen minutes. You can wait if you like. Would you like a cup of coffee?"

"I just had breakfast, so I don't think I will. Thanks anyway."

"There's the Sheriff, now. Sir, this gentleman would like to talk to you."

"Josh, good to see you. Come on to the office, and we can talk. Has there been any more problems?"

"No, Sir, but after the accident that killed my wife and unborn baby boy and put me in the hospital where I was in a coma for two months, I've had dreams of a man. It wasn't every night, but it was shadowy. I knew he was familiar, but I didn't know why. Then the shadows became darker. Last night, I finally saw his face. It was the man who had caused the accident.

I didn't know he had been put in jail until I came out of the coma." Now I know what his face looks like."

"Where did this happen?"

"In Kansas City. We were going to the hospital because my wife was going into labor."

"Let me pull this up on my computer and see what I can find."

He tapped away for a few minutes and said, "Josh, come here and take a look."

Josh went around the computer, "that's him! He's the one that causes the accident! I remember him taking a drink of something, and then he crossed two lanes of traffic and hit us head-on, making the car roll down a hill and crash into some trees. That was the last I knew until two months later."

"There's more here. His name is Dobie Makil. He was in jail for three months then a young woman came to visit him. A couple of days later, he became violently ill, and their doctor said he needed to be taken to the hospital. They put him in an ambulance, but a truck pulled in front of them at four blocks. The truck driver shot the ambulance driver but didn't kill him. Then, another man jumped into the ambulance, released Makil and they escaped. Makil runs a gang that sells drugs and has hired killers at his beck and call. He's wanted in six states but knows how to keep from being caught. I'd bet anything that he's who hired the two to kill you. These are mug shots of all three and I'm betting they are the ones we have to look out for. If you see them, do what you need to do to keep safe."

Chapter 10

Bull and Snake stumbled back to their car and climbed inside. They were hunched over and groaning from the beating they had gotten. They didn't know their opponents would be so powerful. They sat there for several minutes before Bull got the strength to start the car and head back to their hideout. Bull's face was bruised, and he couldn't hear from his right ear. His ribs and back hurt from the heavy walking stick Josh had used on him. Snake was clutching his right wrist and he felt as if he had been tossed in a tumbler. From head to toe, he groaned in pain. "Quit whining," Bull growled. You didn't get beat up any worse than I did. I'll stop at that store, where I got our supplies and get some pain relievers and bandages. They have take-home meals, so I'll get us something to eat. I don't feel like fixing a meal. I just want to lie down. When I stop, pull your hat over your eyes and slump down like you're sleeping."

"What if they ask why you're so beat up?" Snake asked.

"I'll say I was rock climbing, and a boulder broke loose, and I toppled down the embankment. This time of the year, a lot of people do that. I'll bet they see a bunch of climbers who've got hurt."

He went into the store and bought gauze bandaging, pain pills and antibiotic salve. As he checked out, the clerk said, "Man! You must have been climbing rocks somewhere, from the way you look. That's something I don't do. It's just too dangerous for me. I had a friend doing that and he broke both legs and got a concussion." He handed Bull a bottle of liquid and said, "here, take this. Rub it on, and it'll help the bruises. Take care, now."

Bull added the bottle to his purchases and thanked the clerk. Then, he groaningly climbed into the car. When they got to their hideout, he carried in his purchases and started treating their injuries. When he got to Snake's wrist, he shook his head and said, "you're not going to be able to do any shooting with this for at least a month. That guy's wife broke your wrist with that paddle and she may have broken a couple of your ribs, too."

Snake frowned and said, "I can shoot her with my left hand! You just see if I can't!"

Bull laughed and then groaned because laughing hurt. "Yeah, right! You shoot with your left hand like an old granny."

Snake frowned again. "You won't be able to do no better. You can't see out of that one eye, and you can hardly walk. We better call Makil and make up some story about why we haven't done our job. Like, maybe they took a trip, and they haven't come back yet."

"And how are we supposed to explain why we're living in this shack instead of the hotel?"

"Well, Snake said, "we say the cops were hanging around too much and we thought we'd better find a place where they wouldn't look for us after we took down that guy. And what if he comes and sees what we look like? He's gonna know we had trouble. Instead of paying us, he might just give us the lead."

"You're right. We better just keep our mouths shut. If he wants to know anything, he'll probably call us and we can make up some kind of story then."

Josh got home just as Stan walked in the door. He told them what the Sheriff had said and Maud went to her gun closet and got out a rifle. She cleaned it and made sure she had plenty of Ammo. Jake took down a second rifle and made sure it was in good shape. "I live just a couple of doors down and if I hear gunshots, I'll get here to back you up. I don't want any of you to get hurt, especially this gal, he said, giving Maud a hug.

The women began fixing lunch because they knew customers would soon be coming. Josh and Jake just sat back and relaxed. "Jake looked around and said, "I like the looks of the security system security you put in. I want you all to be safe. I've lived around here for a long time and it's like a second home to me. I'd defend Maud with my life."

Josh grinned and said, "I think you think you have feelings for Maud."

"Yeah, that's why I spend a lot of time around here. She's the sweetest, kindest woman I ever met. When I moved here, I went to one of her free holiday meals and saw just what she was like. She likes taking care of people in need. That's why I always make deliveries on those days."

Josh said, "I can see, in your eyes, that you love her. Have you ever asked her to marry you?"

Stan looked down and his cheeks turned red.

"I've thought of it, but maybe I'm just too old for a woman like her. She might not want to get married. She might think I'm just an old fuddy-duddy.

Josh went to him and put his hand on Stan's shoulder. "You're never too old to love someone and if you don't let them know, you're just cheating the one you love and yourself. I think she has some feelings for you, too. I see it in her eyes when she looks at you. It's like when I married Chelsea. I loved my first wife passionately and when she and my unborn died in that accident, I felt like blowing my brains out. I got in my car and just drove, with no destination, in mind. Then, I saw this place and my life changed. I met Chelsea and the more I was around her, the deeper my feelings became until I knew I had to ask her to marry me. Just think it over. Both you and Maud deserve happiness."

Jake sat with his elbows on his knees, but every time he looked up at Maud, Josh could see the love in his eyes. He hoped Jake would get up enough courage to admit he loved her and do something about it.

After dinner was over and cleanup was done, Jake picked up his fiddle and turned to Maud, said "How about a little music? It'll help us all relax."

Josh got his guitar and he and Stan played some soft, relaxing music. It was songs they knew, and Maud began to hum and then she began to sing softly. The tension that had filled the house slowly began to relax. After an hour or so, Stan decided it was time to go home. He gave Maud a kiss on the cheek and a pat on the shoulder. "Take care of yourself. I may see you tomorrow."

Spring was almost in full bloom. Most of the trees were in full leaf. Flowers bloomed along the roads and in people's yards. It wasn't surprising to see people digging to plant new blossoms while others were planting vegetable gardens. Busy people were often humming or singing while they worked and waving at others driving by. Children were at the park, playing on the swings or slides or merry-go-rounds. Farmers were planting crops or tending to their livestock. Birds were singing and building their nests so they could lay their eggs and raise their little ones when the eggs hatched.

At night, Josh and Chelsea would snuggle together in the recliner and watch the ducks swimming in the stream.

"Oh!" Chelsea said. "There's a mama duck and she has ducklings swimming behind her. A-w-w-w, that is so cute! I wish we could go down to the stream, but it's too dangerous. I hope they catch those guys soon, so we can get back to our regular lives."

Josh kissed her and cuddled her closer. "So do I, honey. But, you know, if we wanted to sit outside, we could take a couple of chairs and sit on the other side porch. There's no place those bums could hide to attack us. I think we're going to see a lot of Stan. He's in love with Maud but too chicken to tell her."

Chelsea sat upright and stared at Josh. "Really!" She said. "Really and for sure? How do you know?"

Josh brushed her hair back. "You can see it in his eyes every time he looks at her, but he thinks he's too old for her."

"What! He would be perfect for her. He's a nice person, and I know they'd be good for each other. And I want to sit on the side porch. With the kennels below, I could talk to the dogs and they would warn us if a stranger was around."

"I think that could be arranged, Josh said, but I think it's time we went to bed." He scooped Chelsea up and dumped her on the bed. The next hour or so was spent in cuddling, hugging and kissing.

Chapter 11

In the abandoned house, Bull and Snake were very slowly mending from the injuries they got when they tried to kill Josh and Chelsea. Most of the time, they were lying on the cots, moaning and groaning from pain. Occasionally, Bull had to go to the small nearby store and service station to restock supplies. They were getting so bored that he also picked up some magazines and a deck of cards.

Bull's bruises had almost faded, but the damage to his jaw made it hard to eat and he could have trouble hearing. Most of the day, he spent polishing his rifle and making sure it was in good working condition.

Snake continually complained about his broken wrist and flattened nose. "How am I gonna shoot with this wrist broken and I can hardly breathe with my nose bashed in like it is."

Bull turned to him and said, "Quit whining! I'm getting sick and tired with your bellyaching."

Snake grumbled and said, "If you hurt like I do, you'd be complaining too. That woman beat up on me real good!"

"And you think I didn't get beat up on? All you do is sit around and complain. I'm the one who does everything around here. I go to that store and get more supplies and I'm the one who fixes our meals. I'm the one that hides the car so nobody sees it. You just sit around and gripe. Why don't you try doing a little something? I bought a couple of magazines and a deck of cards. I thought we could play cards once in a while. Make sure your rifle is in good shape. In a couple of weeks, we should be well enough to do our job and when we get it done, we'll call Makil and have him meet us somewhere so we can get paid. We're not going to use the car, either. I'm gonna rent a two-seat motorcycle and it'll be easier to hide in the trees by those rocks. If the cops see it, they'll figure it's just someone practicing their rock climbing and they won't pay any attention to it. We may have to go in more than once until we see those two come out of the house and then, we'll blow their heads off. We'll be gone before the cops can arrive and catch us. We'll dump the bike in the woods, hop on and disappear. The cops will never catch up to us. Then, we'll meet Makil, get our pay and disappear."

Snake thought it over and decided it was a good plan. He grabbed his rifle and started cleaning it. Then, he laid it on a bench by the window and got out his pistol. He cleaned it and made sure he had enough ammunition for it. Two more weeks to wait and then payday.

Josh and Chelsea were sitting on the side porch. It was early evening, and the birds were singing. Maud came out to sit with them, carrying a pitcher of iced tea. Supper was over, the kitchen had been cleaned up, and the front door was locked. It was time to relax, "Ah, she said. It's so nice to just sit and enjoy the evening. The birds are singing. I like this little setting. All it needs is a stool to put your feet on, a cushion to plant your fanny on, and a little table to put your tea glass on. Wish I'd thought about this a long time ago. Don't you think that would have been a good idea?" Chelsea nodded. "I think so. For lunch, we could put small umbrellas over the tables to keep people from getting too hot and at supper, we could fold up the umbrellas so people could see the ducks and enjoy the sunset."

Josh sat back and listened as the women planned and plotted. Then, he went inside and came back with a notepad and pencil. He began sketching and, sometimes, tearing the page off and throwing it away. Then, he would start over. "What do you think of this?" He said as he showed them the sketch. "Instead of umbrellas, we could hang a canopy the length of the porch to keep the rain out and too much sun off customers."

"That's a terrific idea," Maud said. I'll start ordering stuff tomorrow. Then you can start putting it up. I'm glad the two of you are so smart. The sun's setting, so I guess it's time we went in."

When Maud's purchases came, Josh and Chelsea spent the next several days putting everything together. When they were finished, the side porch looked like a beautiful little café. The regular customers, and tourists, wanted to dine on the side porch. There were only a few who chose to stay inside. Children were the most excited because they could peek over the edge and see the dogs in their fenced-in area. They talked to them and sneaked little bites down to them. They were really happy when Bo took them down to see and pet the dogs.

The new side porch café really delighted their customers. They loved being able to sit outside in the cool air and watch the birds and the ducks on the stream.

With parental permission, Bo would get out his sled with wheels, load kids on it and give them a ride around the pasture over the bridge he had built to span from the dock to the opposite bank and into the trees. His advertisement, DOG SLED RIDES FOR CHILDREN, 2:00 p.m. to 5:00 p.m. Monday THRU FRIDAY-25 CENTS PER RIDE, at the side of the road kept him busy. There wasn't a tourist family with children that didn't have to stop so their kids could ride. He earned enough to pay for the training for Rusty and Bella. Of course, after the rides, everyone had to eat so Maud and Chelsea were kept busy cooking and waiting on the customers. At lunch and dinner, Josh got out his guitar to play and sing and Jake was there, almost every day, with his fiddle. Business was rapidly becoming booming. The customers loved it and told others.

While the men were playing, Stan's eyes were always on Maud. Josh could see the love in Stan's eyes and he wished he could persuade him to admit that he loved Maud, but Stan felt he was too old and not good enough for her. He caught Maud glancing Stan's way, too, and he began to wonder if she didn't feel something for him.

As the days went by, tensions eased. The Sheriff still had officers drive by two or three times a day and night. Maud called the Sheriff and told him to have the drive-by officers come in once a day for a meal, and she would leave a sack lunch for the ones who came by at night. "Maud, he said, you are a kind and generous person. I know they will appreciate it."

Maud said, "since you're the boss, I think you should come by at least once a week, don't you?"

He chuckled and said, "When are you having fried chicken?"

"Every Saturday, and I think you should bring your wife. I haven't seen her, except at church, in a month of Sundays. Josh and Stan have been playing some fine music."

"It's a deal. We'll see you Saturday."

When they walked in, Sheriff Barnes and his wife, Peggy. Looked around. "It looks like you are thriving," he said. "That sign Bo put up about the Dog Sled Rides probably draws every tourist with kids."

"It sure does. He's earned enough to get his two dogs trained."

"I'm sure glad he's doing that. We've needed the service of trained dogs for a long time."

"Lunch is ready, Maud said." Do you want to eat inside, or would you like to dine at our new Side Porch Café?"

"What are you talking about?"

"Right this way, Maud said as she led to the door. She opened the door and beckoned them through it. "Our new Side Porch Café."

The Sheriff's mouth dropped open. "How did this come about?"

"Chelsea wanted someplace she could sit, in the cool air, so she and Josh brought out a couple of chairs. Then, I wanted to try it, so I brought out a chair and cushion and the idea just kept growing. Josh installed the canopy so if it rained, nobody would get wet. It rolls down so the wind can't blow rain under it."

"This is incredible! I see a security system has been installed, complete with cameras. Did Josh do that?"

"Yes, he wanted us to be safe. He put deadlocks on all the doors, even where people were staying overnight."

"You're lucky to have a man like him around. Penny, my dear, would you prefer eating inside or outside in the nice new café?"

"H-m-m, my darling, I think I would prefer dining in that lovely new café where I can hear the birds sing." She gave Maud a wink and a grin and headed for the door with her head high and a little shimmy in her hips.

Chelsea went to their table and said, "today's menu is fried chicken, mashed potatoes covered with white gravy and green beans or meatloaf, mashed potatoes with white gravy and green beans and we have chocolate chip cheesecake for dessert. What would you like?"

They both ordered the fried chicken, and he asked for coffee with no sugar or cream while Peggy ordered iced tea. When they had finished their meal, they just sat for a while and enjoyed the peace and quiet. Then, he sighed and said, "Guess it's time to get back to work."

When they went back into the main room, Peggy gave Maud a hug and said, "Thanks for the lunch. You always make the best fried chicken."

"It was my Mama's recipe; she was a really good cook and she taught me all her secrets."

Peggy put her hand on Maud's shoulder and said, "what you're doing for the drive-by officers is beyond kind. They usually have to go to some drive-through place to get something to eat. I know they appreciate what you're doing for them."

"Well, they're protecting us, so the least I can do is see they get a good meal."

Take care of yourselves. Peggy said. Those guys are still out there, and I don't want to see any of you hurt." Then Sheriff Barnes and Peggy left.

The night saw a drastic change in the weather. It was a night when thunder raged. It was right over the Bed and Breakfast and roared and rumbled so loud it made the building shake. It lessened and then came back even louder. Lightning lit up the sky and rain poured, battering the windows. It was a night when it was almost impossible to sleep. Morning was a little better. The thunder still came and went but never seemed to stop. Lightening still flashed and rain still poured. There wasn't even a hint of sunshine.

During a break, in the rain, Josh went out to see what had been scraping the outside wall. He found that a small branch of a nearby tree had broken off and the tips of the limbs were blowing in the wind. He pulled it away from the house and checked for any more problems. When he went back in, Maud, Chelsea and Bo heaved sighs of relief that there was no real damage. For the rest of the day, there were lighter rumbles of thunder and rain came and went. It was chilly, so they had to turn up the heat and Josh and Bo carried wood up from the basement just in case the power went out and they had to use the fireplace for heat and cooking.

Several travelers stopped by to get shelter and a good hot meal. Business wasn't as good as usual, but they served quite a few.

Stan came through the door, bundled is a raincoat. "I ran out of wood and wondered if I could borrow some."

Maud put her hands on her hips and said, "Stan, you don't have to borrow wood. You just stay right here. I have an empty room where you can spend the night and, maybe tomorrow the weather will be better. Then you can worry about wood."

"Maud, me love, you are an angel. Wish I'd thought to bring my fiddle, I'd play some music for you."

She looked out the window and said, "It's just sprinkling right now. Put your raincoat on and run home and get it. I'll soon be having people coming in and I'm sure they would enjoy a little music."

Stan dashed out the door and was soon back. He was just in time because customers were starting to come in. "What about you, Josh? Are you going to play, too?"

"I might as well. I can't let you get the best of me." He got out his guitar and tuned it up.

While the customers were ordering and being served, Jake suggested a little country, and Josh agreed. They agreed on Country Road and started playing. The customers listened avidly and applauded when the song was done. Jake and Josh did a variety of songs and did some singing, too. Everyone enjoyed it and some even stood up and danced.

Maud enjoyed the music and she and Chelsea did a little dancing together between serving the meals.

As people left, they were laughing and dancing out the door. As more came through the door, they smiled and sang along with Jake and Josh. It was a busy and prosperous day. As each drive-by officer came along, they went inside for the meal Maud had promised and they, too, enjoyed the music. The first one took Maud by the hand and danced her around the floor. Every day, Jake and Josh played and sang. Word got around and more people came in. Business was really growing. The night drive-by officers really appreciated the sack lunch Maud left for them because most of the drive-in restaurants were closed by the time they were hungry.

For the next week, there were thunderstorms, showers and partly showers and sunshine, so business wasn't as good, but Jake hung around a lot, and Josh could see the feelings the man had for Maud. Jake was in love but couldn't make himself admit it.

Bull and Snake were becoming very unhappy with their living conditions. The wind broke shingles from the roof and several leaks made it necessary for them to sit close to the heater. When they ran out of fuel, Bull had to bundle up, go to the little store, and buy some more. "I'm getting tired of hanging around here," Bull said. "As soon as this storm is over, we're going down to that bike shop where I can rent a motorcycle. You can drive me down there as long as you keep your cap down so no one can see your face. Then, when we get back, we'll hide the car and the motorcycle under we're ready for it. There are several places we could go out, but there's one place near the town where an elderly couple lives, and they have a garage. We could hide the bike in their garage and make the old double couple do what we say. We could lock them up at night and let the old gal out to cook for us. Then, when we go to take down that couple, we can tie up and gag the old couple, go down to the rocks, and as soon as we do our job, we can take off and disappear someplace where the cops can't find us. Then, we'll call Makil and have him meet us someplace so we can get paid. And, if he tries to do us dirty, we'll blow his brains out and head out of the country. "We might even go down to Mexico and get a nice little place to hang out. The cops won't have a clue about where to find us."

Snake grinned from ear to ear. He liked Bull's plan.

Chapter 12

Officer Tracy Brown knocked on the Sheriff's door. "Come on in." Sheriff Barnes said. "Have a seat. What can I do for you?"

Tracy said, "I live west of here and as I was on the way in, I had an idea. I don't know why I hadn't thought of it before, but there are three or four old houses and several small shops along the way in. One of the houses has a barn built and the house is falling apart, so they wouldn't be fit to live in, but the businesses might have seen the guys you have photos for. If I took the photos and checked at each place to see if anyone had seen those guys, it might give us some clue where they're hiding out."

Sheriff Barnes thought for a minute and then said, that's a good idea, but I don't want you to go alone. I'll send another officer with you as a backup. It's dangerous to do something like that by yourself. I think I'll send Casey Johnson with you. Have you worked with him before?"

Tracy grinned and said. "We've worked together several times. He knows what he's doing and we're pretty good buddies."

The Sheriff picked up the phone and asked Casey to come into his office. He explained what Tracy had suggested, and, with a grin, Casey slapped Tracy on the shoulder. "Good thinking, buddy. We might catch up with those bums before they kill someone. The Sheriff assigned a car for them and sent them on their way.

"Which of us is driving?" Casey asked. "You can drive and I'll show the photos, but we'll both go in together in case we run into trouble."

They started at the new hotel and spoke to the manager. "Sir, have you seen any of these men?"

H-m—m, yes, I've seen all three of them. This one, pointing to the Makil, had one of our finest suites on the third floor. He was well dressed and he stayed in his suite most of the time. He always called to have his meals delivered and ordered a bottle of wine. He seemed to be a very gentlemanly person. Is there some kind of problem?"

"We just need to talk to him, Casey said.

"I'm afraid that is impossible. He said he had some business to take care of and checked out about two weeks ago. I don't know where he was going. These other two had a double room on the first floor. I know they occasionally visited the other gentleman, but they also checked out about the same time."

"Do you have a record of their names"

"Of course. The manager said as he checked the registry. The gentleman in the third-floor suite registered as Daniel Davidson, the tall man on the first floor registered as Amos Archer, and the shorter one was Robert Randall. Is there anything else I can do for you?"

Casey smiled at him and said, "No. They were probably just tourists wanting to stay at your fine hotel. Thanks for your assistance."

As the Officers left, one of the clerks came to the manager and said, "what was that all about?

"I don't know, but with two Officers asking about some of our guests, I hope they hadn't committed any crimes and if they come back, I certainly hope they stay somewhere else."

The two Officers spent the rest of the afternoon going from house to house and business without luck. Finally, Tracy said, "It's almost time for us to get off duty, and I'm getting hungry. Let's stop at that service station. I know they have sandwiches and soft drinks, so maybe we can get something to eat and find out if he's seen any of these guys."

They went inside, spoke to the clerk and showed him the pictures. "Have you seen any of these guys?"

The clerk looked at the pictures and said, "Yeah. This big guy came in about a month ago and bought some camping gear, like cots, blow-up mattresses, a grill, a propane heater, a bunch of canned stuff and bottled water. Man! He looked like someone had beaten the tar out of him. I asked him about it and he said he was rock climbing when a rock broke loose and he fell. Funny, his clothes didn't look like he'd fallen down a bunch of rocks. He was driving a beat-up old car and when he got in to start it, I thought it wasn't gonna start, but it finally did and he headed off toward the crossroad."

While Casey was getting something for them to eat, Track asked, "has this guy been back since?"

"Yeah. He comes about once a week to stock up on food. It's funny, though. This week some guy was driving the car and this guy wanted to rent a motorcycle. I couldn't see what the other guy looked like, but he was smaller and he had his hat pulled down over his face. They both took off toward the crossroad."

Casey laid their food on the counter, paid for it and said, "If this guy comes in again, we'd appreciate it if you called us. Here's a card with the number on it. But be careful that he doesn't know who you're calling. Just pretend you're talking to one of your friends. He's dangerous and we don't want you to get hurt."

"Don't worry about me, I've been leery of that guy since the day I first saw him. He gives me the creeps. Being here all day, and sometimes into the night, made me get myself a license to carry. My gun is under the counter, back far enough that it isn't easy to see. If he tried to cause me any trouble, he'd be in a world of hurt. But, if he saw you guys in your uniforms, he'd probably try to kill you. If you're planning on checking the other side of the road, you won't find much. The first house is falling to pieces. Nobody could live in them. The second house just has rats and snakes. An old man lives in the third house and he carries a shotgun and has a bulldog. Stay outside the screen if you talk to him. He's a crabby old fellow. Next is a fenced-in pasture, which goes downhill and belongs to Jerry Kinks. It's where he runs his cattle. Next is where Thomas Trent makes beautiful wood objects and sells them out front of his place. If you ever want something beautiful, see him. The last house is where the Kinderhooks live. They're an old couple; she makes the best cherry pie you've ever tasted. Her name's Jeanie and she brings me pie every now and then and says I need fattening up. Well, looks like someone needs gas, so I better take care of them. Take care of yourselves. Bye."

"Well, Tracy said, guess it's time to go back to the office and get checked in. I think that young fellow gave us most of what we need to know about the other side of the road." They climbed into their car, ate their sandwiches, and headed back into town. When they got their car put away, they went inside to write their reports and give them to Sheriff Barnes.

The Sheriff read the reports and told them they had done a good job. "Did you check both sides of the road?"

"No, Sir. It was getting late, and the report showed everything over there and he was right. We watched that side of the road and the clerk, at the gas station, there's nothing there anyone could hole up in. I don't think those guys would want to tangle with the old man with the shotgun and bulldog. The only other place is the house at the edge of town, where an elderly couple live. That close to town, those guys would be too easy to spot. We could go up to the crossroad and try it out."

Sheriff Barnes shook his head and said. "There's been a landslide and Roger and Boyd are helping out there. Looks like you two will have to take over their duties until they get back."

"Was anybody hurt, Tracy asked."

"I don't know. I haven't gotten any kind of word yet. I'll sure be glad when we can get a few more officers. Well, you better get home and get some rest. You both may have a busy day tomorrow."

"Yes, Sir. We can handle it."

Casey yawned and stretched. "I'll be glad to get home and relax a little before I get a shower and go to bed."

"Me, too. I feel like I've run a marathon. Meet me at the café and we'll have breakfast before we go to work."

They waved at each other and headed for their cars, happy to be headed home.

Chapter 13

When Bull and Snake got to their hideout, they hid the car and motorcycle in the trees and covered them with a brush. Then, they went back inside their hideout.

"It's clouding up and we might get some rain. If we do, I know those two won't be out in it. I took the bike down toward town and there was a house right close to the trees, near the Climbing Rocks. I saw an older couple out working in their garden. They have a garage and I think we could hide the motorcycle in it and take over the house. The old lady could cook for us and if someone came to the door, we'd tell her to keep quiet, or we'd cut her old man's throat. That would keep her mouth shut. And, if the old man tried anything, we could tie him up and gag him. When things got where we could do our job, we'd tie and gag the old gal and lock her in a closet. Doesn't that sound like a plan?"

"Why not just get rid of them and not mess with all that other stuff?"

"Sometimes I don't think you have a brain in your head. If people don't see her out in her garden, once in a while, they might come over and see if something is wrong. I'd let her go out there and work while I watched from inside the doorway. She'd know what we'd do to her old man if she tried anything."

Snake chuckled. "I see what you mean. We're in control and they can't do anything about it. After we do our job, we make sure they can't tell anyone about us and we take off. The cops would never find us. We could just relax as long as we watched the old folks. I like it."

Bull flopped down on a cot and put his hands behind his head. "We better check and see if they have a cellar they can't get out of. Then, we could lock them in at night and tell them what will happen if we hear them holler for help. I wonder if the old gal is a good cook. I'd sure like to have a good, home-cooked meal." "Me, too. That stuff we've been eating fills you up, but it isn't like having a real meal. When we went over to that Halloween shindig they had, the food was really good. But what about when we go to the rocks? What do we do with them then?"

"We tie 'em up and put them in the cellar if they have one. If they don't, we tie and gag em and lock 'em in a closet. When we get our job done, we hop on the bike and take off before anyone can catch us. I might even leave a little joke on the door that says, Look in the closet or (cellar) for a nice surprise. Can you imagine the look on their faces when they see those people tied up and gagged?"

Both Bull and Snake laughed heartily. "It's stopped raining' so we can take off and get things done. We don't need to take anything with us except our clothes and personal belongings. We don't want to leave anything to identify us."

"Yeah, Snake said, just think how nice we are, leaving all this stuff for the next person who has to live here." He and Bull laughed heartily at Snake's joke.

"A-www! It was such a nice place to live in. The roof leaked, so we could take a shower and we had a grill to cook on. It was like living in a mansion." They roared with laughter as they took off for the house near town.

They wore their helmets, so no one could identify them and parked the motorcycle behind the garage, where it would be hidden. Then, guns drawn, they knocked on the back door. The lady of the house saw them and clapped her hand against her chest. "W-w-hat do you want?" "Just back up and you'll find out what we want. Both of you just sit down and listen. Bull said. We're taking over this place and you're going to do what we tell you. We won't shoot you because it would cause too much noise, but we will cut your throats. That's nice and quiet." Pointing at the woman, he said, "you'll cook our meals and do anything else we need and you, old man, will just quietly sit and watch TV. Any yelling for help or trying to escape and you're both dead. Understand?" They both nodded their heads. "Good! We'll put our motorcycle in your garage and you, Ma'am, I'll allow you to work in your garden occasionally, but I'll be watching every move you make and if you try anything, you know what will happen to your hubby. Do you have a cellar?" The woman said," It's where I keep what I can from the garden."

"Snake, go check it. You know what I'm looking for."

Snake went down the steps, looked over everything carefully, and then came back up. "It's perfect. "he said. "No way out except this door."

"You watch them while I put the motorcycle away." Bull said as he left Snake guarding them at gunpoint.

In a few minutes, he came back in. "Everything is secure. Now, Ma'am, it's about supper time. What are you fixing tonight?"

She rubbed her hands together, I have a beef roast in the oven and some potatoes baking, and I made brownies this afternoon. Do you want coffee?"

"That sounds very nice, Ma'am and we would like coffee. You're being very cooperative. As long as you stay that way, you'll be just fine."

Bull and Snake settled into comfortable chairs and relaxed but kept an eye on the old couple. "Say, Ma'am, what's your name? Calling you Ma'am gets a little tiresome."

"My name is Mildred and my husband is Tom."

"Now, isn't that a lot friendlier? Well. Mildred and Tom, you do what we tell you and when we tell you and you'll be fine as a frog's hair. Don't and you're likely to get hurt or worse, understand? "

I don't know how long we'll be here. It may be a couple of days or a couple of weeks. It depends on how long it takes to do our job.

Bull stood up and stretched. "I'm getting tired. I think it's time to hit the hay. Into the cellar, folks. Snake, get a mattress, a couple of pillows and some blankets. We wouldn't want our hosts to get sick, would we? I'll lock the door and if I hear any yelling for help, I'm going to be very upset with you."

Tom laid out the mattress and Mildred spread the blankets. Then, they crawled in and snuggled together. "What are we going to do? Tom whispered in her ear. "I don't know," she said, "those two are evil. They carry guns. The big one said they had a job to do and I'll bet it'll be crooked. Maybe when they get it done, they'll leave." "But will we be dead or alive? Tom said. "You know, this reminds me of when we were younger, and we'd snuggle up and make love. Maybe that's what we should do now. It might be our last chance."

Mildred giggled, put her arms around his neck and held him close. 'I love you, Old Man. She kissed him and ran her hands over his body.

Bull peeked through the door. "Look at that! They're like a couple of kids making love. I guess you're never too old for it." He said with a lecherous chuckle.

He stretched and yawned. I think I'll get ready to hit the sack. How about you, Snake? It's still raining, so are you going to sleep in a bed or out here, on the couch?"

"I think I'll stay here and watch some TV. I haven't watched it in a long time."

Good idea. Then you can hear them if they start yelling. You can come to get me and I'll take care of the problem."

The next morning, Bull unlocked the door and yelled down the stairs. "Up and at it. It's time for breakfast."

Mildred and Tom crawled out of the covers and made their way up the steps. "Is it alright if I wash my face and comb my hair?"

"There's a sink in the kitchen, do it there. What are you going to fix for breakfast?"

"I thought about scrambled eggs and bacon with homemade biscuits, gravy, and coffee if that's all right with you. And I thought you might like grilled ham and cheese sandwiches and potato salad, with apple pie and ice cream, for lunch. For supper, I was going to take the leftover beef roast and make beef stew with more apple pie and ice cream for dessert. I just want to keep you happy, so you won't want to hurt us."

Bull gave her a smile and said, "Ma'am, with the way you cook and if you don't try any shenanigans, I won't harm a hair on your head. Do you understand that?"

"Oh, yes, Sir! We'll do whatever you say, won't we, Tom?"

That afternoon, Mildred did their laundry and made the beds, treating Bull and Snake more like guests than a pair of hired killers. After supper was over and the dishes done, Bull sent Mildred and Tom back to the cellar and locked the door. Then, with a contented sigh, Bull stretched out on the couch. "This has been a pleasant day, good food, clean laundry and a chance to relax. If it isn't raining tomorrow, after breakfast, we'll put those two back in the cellar, get the rifles and head for the rocks to see if the two we're supposed to take down are out. If they aren't, we'll have to come back and wait."

"You're right, Snake said. We've had a good couple of days, but I want to get our job done and get paid. I wonder why we haven't heard from Makil. You don't suppose he's taken off on us, do you? I think he's just the kind that would."

Chapter 14

Unaware of the danger lurking not far from them, Josh and Chelsea went about their daily business, helping Maud with the cooking, sweeping and dusting, and cleaning the rooms where guests had spent the night. Jake was there frequently. He helped Maud with cooking and cleaning up. He waited on the tables in the Side Porch Café, helped Bo with his dogs and, and at dinner, he played his fiddle while Josh played his guitar. The new Side Porch Cafe and the music boosted Maud's business greatly.

When dinner was over and the cleanup was done, Josh, Chelsea, Maud and Jake sat in the Side Porch Café and listened to the music of the night. There were peeper frogs singing their night songs, the distant hooting of owls and the soft whisper of leaves softly rustling in the trees. "I'm glad we put this here, Chelsea said. It's so peaceful. We haven't had any problems in quite a while. Do you think those men who attacked us have given up and left the country?"

Josh kissed her cheek and said. "I doubt it. Those two were hired killers and I'm sure the man who hired them is the one who caused the accident that killed my wife and baby boy. He was put in jail, but he got out somehow, and he wants revenge for being put in jail. They're still around somewhere, so we really have to be careful."

Jake scooted a little closer to Maud and Josh and Chelsea smiled. They knew he was in love with Maud. It was a matter of getting him to admit it to her.

Josh said, "You know, I'm thinking about getting a piece of sheet metal and putting it on the side of the back porch that's toward the Climbing Rocks. That's the most likely direction an attack would come from. The rain has probably kept them in, so things should be quiet for a little while, but it's supposed to be clear by tomorrow afternoon."

They didn't know just how close danger really was. Bull and Snake were grumbling about Mildred and Tom was locked in the cellar with Mildred's voice close to Tom's ear. "I have a plan," she whispered. "Tomorrow is Wednesday and Sally always calls on Wednesday and when the phone rings, those two won't want me to answer it, but I'll tell them. If I don't, she will send someone over to see if everything is all right. I'm going to say her Uncle Claude, and that kid of his, is coming to stay for three or four weeks."

"But honey, Sally doesn't have an Uncle Claude!" "I know and Sally knows, but those two crooks don't know. Just go along with what I tell her."

The next morning, Bull let Mildred and Tom out of the cellar and waited while she fixed breakfast. They were both pacing around and grumbling and groaning because it was still raining and they couldn't get out to see if Josh and Chelsea were where they could be seen.

When Mildred had fed them and cleaned up the kitchen, she started sweeping and dusting. Suddenly, the phone rang and, when she started to reach for it, Bull said, "Don't answer that phone!"

Mildred put her hand up to her mouth and then said, "It's our daughter. She always calls on Wednesday to see how we are, and if nobody answers, she sends Marybeth over to check on us. And when she comes, she talks a mile a minute and doesn't know when to shut up."

Bull gave a heavy groan and said, "Answer it, but don't say anything about us, or else!"

Mildred picked up the phone, "Hi, honey, it's good to hear from you." "Same here, Mom. How's Dad doing." "Pretty good. He's over his cough, but I've got some bad news for you. Your Uncle Claude phoned and said he and that brat kid of his were coming and planning to stay three or four weeks. You know I can't stand that man! He drinks and smokes and that is bad for your Dad. He swears all the time and throws things around. I don't want him in this house!" "Mom, I don't have an Uncle Claude." "I know, and you know how men like him are. You're the only one he'll listen to. Call him and tell him I don't want him here." "Mom, is there someone that shouldn't be there?" "Yes, there is." "Are you in danger?" Yes, we are." "I'll call the Sheriff and, when it's safe, call me back right away." "Okay, goodbye, Sweetie." She hung up and told Tom that Marybeth made sure Claude wouldn't come.

"So, who is this Claude? Bull asked."

"He's our daughter's uncle in-law and he's a hateful rat, but Sally is the only one he'll listen to. Tom, come help me change the sheets in the bedrooms. Guys, I'm going to set your bags just out the door because I'm going to do a lot of cleaning in the rooms, and I don't want to get your things dusty and dirty. Is that okay?"

That's fine, Bull said.

Mildred and Tom shook out the sheets, and she reached for a pillow. She put her mouth close to his ear and whispered,

"Marybeth called the Sheriff's office and they'll come right away. When we see them through the window, we'll shut and lock the door. I secretly unlocked the front door while those two were eating. Here they come! Get the door shut and locked!"

Snake was heading for the recliner when he glanced out the front window. "Bull!" He shrieked. "Grad your stuff. The cops are coming!" They grabbed their bags and ran into the garage. Bull grabbed the rifles, they mounted the motorcycle and fled out the back garage door and down the bard wire slope along the cow-filled pasture. "We'll head for those trees. The cop cars can't follow us down the slope. They'll have to go clear up to the cross road and by the time they turn, we'll be well hidden in the trees. We'll keep going, up through the trees, until it's too far for them to search. We'll have to find a new place to hole up and, then I'll think of something."

"Are you folks all right, an officer asked. Do you recognize any of these men?"

Mildred and Tom looked at the pictures and pointed out Bull and Snake. "We did everything they told us to do because we were afraid they'd hurt us or kill us. They made us sleep in the cellar so we couldn't escape."

"And how did you manage to call us?"

"Our daughter calls us every Wednesday and when I reached for the phone, the tall guy told me not to answer it, but I told him, if I didn't, she would have Marybeth come and see if everything was all right and Marybeth talks a blue streak. Then, I made up a story about a fictitious Uncle named Claude, who I said was a real rat and I didn't want him coming and staying for a month because he smokes and drinks and swears a blue streak. Sally knows she doesn't have an Uncle Claude and she asked if there was someone in the house that shouldn't be here and I said there was. Then she asked if we were in danger and I said yes. She said she would hang up and call you guys right away. While they were eating breakfast, I sneaked over and unlocked the front door so you could get in. Tom and I pretended we were going to change the sheets and when we saw you, we shut and locked the bedroom door."

Chief Officer Johnson burst into laughter. "Ma'am, you are a clever woman. We can't chase after them because of the slope behind your house, so; we'll go to the crossroad and search from that direction since they were headed for the trees. One of us will stop by every day to be sure there's no trouble. Be careful and keep your doors locked unless you know who's there."

When they were gone, Mildred called her daughter so she wouldn't worry. "Mom," Sally said, "Why don't you and Dad come stay with us for a while? You know how Tommy loves playing games with his Grandpa and I miss you. You haven't visited in quite a while. They could go fishing and we could go up to Book Cliffs and see all the fossils of the sea creatures embedded in the rocks. Please say you'll come."

"I'll talk it over with your Dad and I'm sure he'll say we'll come. We miss you, too. Bye, for now, sweetie."

"Bye, Mom. Give Dad a kiss for me."

They hung up and Mildred told her what Sally said. Then she said, "you know, Tom, there isn't much here for us. What would you think about selling this place and moving to Grand Junction? We would be close to family."

Tom thought for a minute and said, "The last time we were there, I liked it. The people were friendly, Tommy and I could go down to the river and go fishing and I liked that little Quaker Church we went to. We could get a place big enough for you to have a garden and for me to have a workshop. I could teach Tommy how to make things out of wood and we could set up a little shop where we could sell what we make. Mildred was excited and she said, "I could crochet afghans and booties and baby things and sell them in the shop. People like homemade things. I'll Call Sally and tell her to look around for a place for us."

Mildred called Sally and told her their plans. She heard whooping and hollering. "Really, really, Mom? I've hoped you would for such a long time." When Sally told Tommy, Mildred heard him jumping around and shouting in glee.

Chapter 15

Bull and Snake disappeared into the heavy trees. "What if it rains? What are we going to do?"

Bull concentrated on his driving and said, "I don't know, but we'll figure something out. Keep watch for where we might find some shelter. I think there's a gravel road just a little farther ahead. I don't think there are many people along there, but sometimes there are old sheds and shacks where we could hole up for a couple of days. Keep a watch, just in case." Bull cruised along the edge of the trees until he reached the gravel road. He started to go past it, but Snake yelled and pointed down the road. "Look, there's a house down the road, and I see some cows. I don't see any other houses, so that must be the only one. Let's check it out."

"I'll see if there's anyone there, and if there is, I'll talk to them. You just go along with what I say."

He drove down the road and into a gravel driveway just as an elderly man came out of the barn.

The old man gave them a wave and a smile. When he got to the motorcycle, he said, "Howdy. Anything I can do for ya?"

Bull dismounted and looked at the cattle. "Looks like you have some nice livestock. My name is Marty Chance and this other guy is Kyle Kelton. I used to work with my Dad on our farm. I see you have some horses, too. I liked working with him until he passed away and I had to sell the farm. Whenever I see a place like this, I think about our farm and I get to feeling sad. My friend never worked a farm, but he's a good mechanic."

"Come on in the house and we can talk. I've got a pot of stew on the stove and you're welcome to share a meal with me."

He escorted them in and got them seated around the table. "Do you like coffee?"

"One of my favorite drinks," Bull said.

"Good. I'll put on a pot. By the name, my name's Dan Douglas, but folks just call me Pops. My wife and I lived here around forty years until she passed away, I never did have kids to give it to. I'm planning on selling' this place and the livestock. I'm getting too old to do it by myself. Hired hands are few and far between. Seems nobody wants to work a farm anymore."

"That's sure the truth, Bull said. Kyle and I have been looking for work, but all we can find barely keeps us fed. I have an idea. I'd love to do the farm work and Kyle could take care of the equipment and, maybe, feed the chickens. What do you say, pops? We could get this place back in shape, and you wouldn't have to sell it. You could pay us what you can so we can buy things we might need, like clothes and boots and a coat for winter. We know you love this place. It would be good for all of us. What do you say?"

Dan thought for a minute and then said, "I think it's a great idea. It's been lonely around here. I don't have any neighbors and the only time I'm around people is when I go to the grocery store or gas up one of the vehicles. There are two bedrooms on the left of the hall and the bathrooms at the end of the hall. Sheets and towels are in the closet across from the bedrooms.

Bring in your stuff and take your pick of the two bedrooms. It's gonna be great having someone to talk to once in a while."

Bull and Snake went to get their gear. "I didn't know you ever did farming," Snake said.

"I helped my Dad when I was a kid, Bull said. "We had cows, pigs and chickens. Then he bought a couple of horses and it was my job to clean their stalls, feed them and groom them. You know! I enjoyed it. Then, Dad got sick and died and I was put in a shelter. I didn't like that, the other kids teased me because I was big so I ran away and they never did catch me. I got in with a tough street gang and that's when Makil took me into his group. He had one of his guys teach me how to steal, pickpocket, attack people and take what they had. One of his crew taught me how to use a gun. I got pretty good with a handgun and a rifle."

"Yeah," Snake said. "My old man was a junkie, but he was a smart guy. He taught me how to hot wire a car or, if the customer left a key, so it could be moved, I'd make a duplicate key so one of the crew could steal the car after it was taken home. That way, I never got in trouble. They also taught me how to shoot. I got a real reputation for the way I could handle a gun of any kind."

They carried their gear inside and chose a bedroom. Dan was busy in the kitchen frying hamburger to make a pot of spaghetti.

"Come on in and have a seat," Dan said," I have a pot of spaghetti, salad and breadsticks and there's ice cream in the freezer. Eat all you want and then we'll talk."

After eating, they went into the living room and sat down. Dan sat, with his elbows on his knees and looked from one man to the other. "I don't have a lot of money, but I could pay each of you $150 a month. Is that acceptable?"

Bull looked at Snake and said, "With what we've been able to earn, it's like a fortune. I can take care of the cattle and horses and do some fence mending. Kyle can take care of the chickens and the machinery. He's real good with machines. Are you planning to sell any of the livestock?"

"There's a riding school that wants to buy a couple of horses, but it'll be a month or so before they're ready. I'm planning to sell a few cows, but there's one that's about ready to drop her calf and she'll need some extra watching. She sometimes has problems when she calves."

Bull grinned and said, "I've done that before with my Dad. She had the prettiest calves, but boy, did she have problems getting them out. I'll keep a close watch on her. If there's a store somewhere nearby where we earn some money, we need to get some new jeans and shirts and maybe some bill caps. Our clothes are getting pretty worn out."

Dan smiled and said, "The only store is about five miles down the road, and they only sell groceries, but I have a catalog. Give me a list of what you need and your sizes, and I'll order it and take it out of what I pay you. It only takes three or four days to get an order from them." Oh, you should put your bike in the barn, or you're liable to come out and find your selves sitting in a pile of bird poo. He laughed and said, I had a motorcycle once and I can't tell you how often the seat of my pants was covered with it."

Bull said, "Glad you reminded me. I'll put it in the barn right now and then check on the cattle, especially the one that's about ready to drop her calf." He headed out the door and motioned Snake to follow him.

"What am I supposed to do? I don't know anything about animals and why are you having him order those clothes? I never wear anything like that and neither do you."

Bull walked the bike into the barn and told Snake, "The bike's hidden and there's a big bag of chicken feed against the well. You can feed the chickens. Just get a bucket, and fill it up. Then, take your hand and scatter it in the pen and I think you can figure out how to make sure they have plenty of water in that container over there. As far as the clothes go, if someone drives by and sees us in jeans, checkered shirts and bill caps, they'll just think we're a couple of farmhands and they won't pay any attention to us. I think we should try to get hold of Makil and let him know what's been happening. We'll work for a couple of weeks to earn some money. I'll tell the old man we got a phone call that said a friend was hurt in an accident and we'd like to take a day off to check on him, but we'd be back before dark. Then, we'll head back to the Climbing Stones and see if the guy we're supposed to take down is out where we can get to him."

They worked hard. Bull helped the cow drop her calf and found he was enjoying himself. It reminded him of the times he had worked with his Father. Snake fed the chickens and got so he enjoyed it when they came running at feeding time. Sometimes he'd stick his fingers through the fence and chuckle when they pecked at them.

Bull grinned and said, "You seem to enjoy feeding the chickens.'

"Yeah, it's funny when they come running when they see the feed bucket. They cackle and if I put my fingers through the wire, they nibble at them and make little crooning noises. I think I like chickens. I'm going to start checking out the equipment. There's a delivery truck in the barn, and I want to make sure it's running. The cops know we have a motorcycle. We could load the bike in the truck so it couldn't be seen. We can ask the old man if we can borrow his pickup to go see your 'phony' friend. Then, we can park in the trees and climb the rocks to see if the guy we're supposed to take down is where we can get to him. I'm going to paint a company sign on the side of the truck and paint over the license plate and change the numbers so if we have to use it, the cops won't be able to track it."

Bull grinned and slapped him on the back. "That's a great idea', he said. "If it works out right, we can try to get hold of Mavil and set up a meeting place so we can get paid."

After work that evening, Bull talked to Day. "Could we borrow your truck after our days' work, so we can go see our friend? He's doing better, but he's still in bad shape. He doesn't have any family and I know he gets lonely. We'll keep gas in it and be back close to supper."

Dan said, "Use it when you need it, but I'll be leaving in a little bit. It's my granddaughter's birthday and we're having a barbeque for her. I'll be gone all day tomorrow and staying the night, so I won't be back until the next morning. There's plenty of food in the freezer, so you won't go hungry. You can go with me if you want. You can use the truck if you need to."

Bull stretched and said, "Thanks, but I think we'll just get our chores done and then relax and watch a little TV. There's supposed to be some pretty good games tomorrow. Be careful on the road and tell your granddaughter we wish her a happy birthday."

Chapter 16

Stan was spending the day helping Josh do some maintenance around the Bed and Breakfast. The hard winter storm and the heavy spring rain had done some damage. There needed to be some painting done, tiles needed to be replaced in two or three of the bedrooms and the foundation needed cementing in spots to keep water from running into the basement. Some of the basement shelving needed to be replaced so Maud could store the fruit and berries she canned and Chelsea was learning to make jams and jellies that would also go on the new shelving. She and Maud whistled and sang while they worked. Spring was in the air and they felt it clear to their bones.

"You know, Maud," she said. "I used to watch you canning and making jellies and I never realized how satisfying it is. Just knowing you made it yourself, and it tastes so good, is amazing. Now that I'm a married woman, what are you going to teach me next?"

"H-m-m! How would you like to learn to quilt? Some of my pals and I used to get together on weekends after I closed for the day, set up our frames and quilt like crazy. We haven't done it for a couple of years, but I'll bet they'd like to get back into it."

"Did you do the covers on the beds?"

"Most of them, but there's also crochet, embroidery, tatting, and knitting. There are a bunch of things you could try. When you've done something yourself, if it's beautiful or ordinary, you feel good about it because you did your best. Well, since it's an off day, I guess we'd better get some sandwiches made and get the boys off the roof so we can have some lunch. I'm starting to get hungry. We can sit in the Side Porch Café and listen to the birds singing while we eat. Go yell at them, and I'll get the sandwiches started."

Chelsea went out the door and yelled. "Hey, guys, come on down. Maud is making lunch and we're going to eat out here, in the Café. Jake, Josh and Bro scrambled down the ladder and rushed to claim a table where they could all sit together.

Chelsea went back in to help Maud. On the plates, they put toasted ham and cheese sandwiches, a scoop of potato salad and a dill pickle. Maud took the plates out while Chelsea carried iced tea and napkins. Bo and Jack sat with Maud between them.

It was a beautiful day. While they ate, they listened to the birds and laughed as a squirrel ran up with a nut that cracked and ate. Then, it ran back down for another nut.

"He's a hungry little fella," Josh said, with a chuckle.

The dogs started barking at it and it looked over the branch and chattered at them as if it was saying, "ha, ha you can't get me. Then, it climbed a little higher and, in a notch between two branches, settled down for a nap. They couldn't help laughing at the little fellow's boldness. They finished their lunch with a dish of chocolate chip cookie dough and then the men decided to finish their job while the ladies cleaned up the dishes.

When everything was ship shaped, Maud called one of her friends. When the friend answered, she said, "Hello." "Jessica, it's me." "Maud! Is it really you? The only place I see you anymore is at church. How are you doing?"

"I'm doing fine. Business is really doing well. The reason I called is because Chelsea wants to learn to quilt and I thought about how a group of us used to get together, after church, and spend the afternoon quilting and talking and how much we enjoyed it. I called you first and I wondered if you would be willing to call some of the others and see if they would like to get together like we used to. We always had so much fun and we could teach Chelsea how to quilt. She's so ambitious; she wants to learn all kinds of things." "I'll be happy to call," Jessica said. "Margaret was talking about that the other day. She really misses it. When would you want to start?"

"Well, Maud said, most of the repair work is done, so how about next Sunday after church?"

"That sounds good. I'll call you after I talk to the others. Take care."

Maud told Chelsea about the plan and she was so excited she danced around the floor and gave Maud a big hug.

When the men came in from finishing, Chelsea told Josh about Maud's plan, and he hugged her because she was so happy. Then, he gave Maud a hug and thanked her.

It was almost time for evening service at the church, so they all changed, piled into their vehicles, and headed out. When they got there, Maud talked to some of her friends and three were excited. They had missed their get-together. The other two had moved and were no longer in town. They scheduled a time, and Jessica gave Chelsea a hug and said, "I hear you want to learn how to quilt."

Chelsea clapped her hands in glee. "Oh, yes! I've seen people doing all kinds of handicrafts. I've always wanted to learn but never had the opportunity."

"Well, now's your chance. Clara crochets Afghans and all kinds of baby things, and Nicole embroiders the most beautiful scarfs and pillowcases you ever saw. She loves doing wildlife and Betty knits sweaters you'd swear came out of some fancy boutique. I know you're going to have fun. We'll see you next Sunday after church."

Chelsea was so excited; she chattered all the way home. When they all got to the Bed and Breakfast, they grabbed a snack and some iced tea and went to sit at the Porch Side Café to relax, listen to the night birds and tree frogs and gaze at the stars.

Chelsea had her head against Josh's shoulder and hummed a little song. Then she pointed and said, "I'd like to build a house right over there. I'd be close enough to help Maud, and, at night we could sit on the porch and watch the moon rise; it would be our own little home."

"Honey, we'll have that house when those killers, and their boss, are caught."

"Do you think they're still around?" "I know they are. I can feel it. Their boss wants revenge for being put in jail after the accident that killed my wife and unborn baby. They'd kill me, but I'm afraid of what they might do to you. You're a beautiful woman and they wouldn't hesitate to take advantage of you and when they had satisfied themselves, they would probably kill you. That's why I want you to be very, very careful. I'm going to put that metal sheet on the Climbing Rocks side of the back porch. That seems to be where most of the trouble comes from. Jack is going to give me a hand with it."

"Josh, Stan is in love with Maud, isn't he?

'The way he looks at her, and I think she feels the same. Why doesn't he tell her how he feels? And I can sense that she feels lonely sometimes. When he's here, she fixes his favorite meals and she laughs more when he's around. I think they'd be good for each other.

"I've talked to him about it and he thinks he's too old for her and he isn't good enough. He comes over here to be near her, but he doesn't have enough nerve to bring up the subject. I guess all we can do is give him some time. The more he's around her, the stronger his feelings will become."

"It makes me so sad when I see the way he looks at her!"

Josh kissed her forehead and held her close. "I know, Love, but we can't do anything about it. I think it's time we crawled into bed and did some hot and heavy snuggling. What do you say to that?"

Chelsea gave him a sexy look and headed for the bedroom. Once inside, she unbuttoned her blouse and slowly let it slide off her shoulders. Then, she slowly unbuttoned his shirt and slipped it down his arms. "I haven't had any hot and heavy snuggling; all day and I think you should make up for it."

Josh gave her a devilish smile and began to undress her. "I think my beautiful wife should help her handsome husband get undressed, too. Don't you?"

Soon, they were in bed, snuggled close together, arms around each other, lip to lip. Josh looked deep into her eyes and said, "When my wife and baby were killed, I thought I would never marry again. When I saw the sign outside, I decided to have a meal, spend the night and take off again. I didn't know where I was going, and I didn't care. If I had run off a cliff, it wouldn't have mattered. I didn't even know I was in Colorado. I was trying to outrun the pain. But, when I saw you, something happened; the pain lessened. You were so beautiful and gentle and kind. I decided to stay another night, and another, and another until I didn't want to leave. The longer I was here, the more I wanted to be with you. When we were attacked by those men at the stream, if they had hurt you, I would have done my best to kill them. Josh laughed and said, "I remember the look on that little guy when you slammed him across the face with the canoe paddle and then tried to beat the stuffing out of him with it. He sure didn't waste any time getting away from you.

Chelsea gave him a hug and a kiss and said. "We make a pretty good team. Remember the night those two tried to sneak up to the house and the dogs started barking? Bo let Rusty and Bella, and a couple more dogs out, and they attacked those two guys. They tried to fight them off but then started screaming like banshees and running. I don't think they had guns, or they would have tried to shoot the dogs, but all they wanted was to get to the Climbing Rocks and escape. Bo gave a whistle and the dogs all came running back and into their pens as if nothing had happened. I'm surprised those guys would try anything else. They always get the worse end of it."

"They're getting paid for it," Josh said, "and they'll risk anything to get paid."

Josh pulled the coverlet up around their shoulders, tucked her head under his chin, warmed his hands in her flame-red hair, and stroked her silky soft skin. Then sleep crept over them and they dreamed of love, joy and happiness.

The next morning, Josh and Stan hefted the sheet metal and started pushing it to the back door porch. Chelsea was standing at the doorway, watching as they worked. Josh was on the pulling end and partly out the door when he glanced over his shoulder and saw a bright flash of light. "Get down!" he yelled as he pushed Chelsea to the floor and flung his body over hers. Then, there was the ping of shots hitting the metal.

Maud and Stan ran to the gun locker, and each grabbed a rifle and a box of shells. Then, they ran back to the porch and both laid down rapid fire toward the Climbing Rocks. Bo came running up the basement stairs. "Call the Sheriff." Maud yelled as they continued pumping shots toward the rocks. One shot from the attacker's ricochet caused a crease across Maud's shoulder, but she kept up a barrage of shots. Then, a short, chunky man tumbled out of the rocks and struggled to get into a shelter. A tall, husky man scrambled down, grabbed the other man by the shirt and dragged him up behind the rocks. Then Maud and Stan saw them running into the trees to escape.

Stan grabbed a towel and was holding it tightly to the crease when an Officer came into the room, "is anyone hurt?" he asked. Stan turned to the Officer and said. "Maud got a crease across her arm. Thank God it wasn't worse. I couldn't stand it if she got hurt badly."

Josh stood up and gave Maud a grin. "I didn't know you could shoot like that," he said.

Maud gave him one eyebrow-up look, put her fists on her hips and said, "Son, my Dad taught me to shoot when I was ten years old and I haven't forgotten any of it. This puny scratch doesn't matter one bit. I'll just put a band-aid on it and forget it."

Stan was still holding the towel to her arm, tears in his eyes. "It would have mattered to me a lot," he said. "If you'd been hurt bad, it would have killed me. I know I'm an old man and not worth much, but you mean a lot to me. I've been putting this off for a long time, but I have to say it. I love you, Maud. I have for a long time, but I was scared to tell you. I was afraid you'd think I was just a stupid old man and you wouldn't want me. I'd die if anything happened to you." He turned away, but Maud took him by the shoulder and said, "I wondered when you'd tell me. I've been waiting a long time. Every time you come in that door, I wonder if it'll be now."

I thought you were too good for me. Stan said. Maud, will you consent to be my wife forever and forever?"

Maud put her arms around him and gazed into his eyes. "You don't know how long I've waited to hear you say that. I've known you for a couple of years and you've grown on me. Every time you've given me a grin or patted my shoulder, it's grown deeper and I wanted you to tell me."

"Why didn't you say anything?"

"Because. My Love, guys are supported to be the ones to do the courting. Not the girls."

Everyone was grinning and then shouting with joy. Chelsea hastily bandaged the scratch on Maud's and then hugged her while the men were all shaking hands. The Sheriff came in with a look of puzzlement on his face. "We weren't able to catch those guys," he said. "But what's going on here?" When they told him the good news, he hugged Maud and gave Stan a hearty handshake.

"Those two had their escape route well thought out, the Sheriff said. "There are so many turn-offs, we couldn't spot which way they went. We have a system of cameras that will send an alert if anyone is spotted going toward the Climbing Rocks and we have volunteers to watch the cameras. If they see someone they don't recognize, we'll have a chance to spot those two. Stay close to home and if you need to go anywhere, call us and I'll send an Officer with you. I don't want any of you hurt. Now, let's talk about the important part. I take it; there's a wedding in the planning. When and where? I'm glad it's finally happening. When I've been here for lunch, I've seen you two making googol eyes at each other and neither of you realized you were doing it. You know, I play the bagpipe and would be happy to play the Wedding March for you."

"As soon as we get everything arranged, we'll let you know."

Stan said, "It would be nice if some of your off-duty Officers could act as ushers in uniform. I was a cop years ago, and they did that, and it really made things special to see the uniformed officers getting people seated and, then, bringing in the Groom, to walk down the aisle."

Chelsea thought it over and said, "I can see it. With Maud's approval, I could be the bridesmaid, Josh could be the Groomsman and Bo could have Bella carrying the pillow with the ring. Maud, I can see you in a beautiful silk dress, with a crown of flowers in your hair and carrying a beautiful bouquet. And the officers, in their uniforms, escorted everyone to their seats. Then, the bagpipe starts the wedding in March and Stan walks up the aisle and stands beside you. *In my mind, it seems so wonderful it makes me want to cry.* Just think it over. It's your wedding, and I want you to be happy. We could set the dining room up for the cake and the food."

With tears streaming down her face, Maud wrapped her arms around Stan and said, "I love you so much. When do you want to get married?"

"How about the end of the month," he said. "I know about a beautiful place in the mountains. There's a babbling brook and an incredible waterfall. Right now, the flowers are in bloom and sometimes, you see a deer crossing the stream with her fawn behind her. Would that suit you, Maud?

"I haven't gotten into the mountains very often, and it sounds wonderful. But who's going to take care of things while I'm gone?

Chelsea hugged Maud and said, "Don't worry. Josh and I and Bo will take care of everything. I'm not as good a cook as you are, but we'll see that none of the guests will go hungry, and Carrie Ann and Josie have volunteered to waitress. We'll see that everyone is taken care of."

Chapter 17

Bull and Snake read about the wedding and knew Josh would be there. The newspaper had announced the time and place, so they decided to disguise themselves and go down by the church to see if there was a place they could hide. They didn't care how many people would be there, just so they would be able to get a clear shot at Josh and then escape. The lawn at the side of the church had large trees and thick, flowering shrubs that were the perfect place to hide.

The next three weeks were as busy as a zoo. The wedding was to be at the church, on the beautiful back lawn. The only flowers to be bought were those for Maud's bouquet, the crown on her head, and the flower girls. The women from the church were busy getting the decorations for the dining room and the chairs and tables set up. Maggie Blumbaum was going to make the cake, and since she was a professional baker, it would be beautiful. Then, on a Sunday afternoon, Chelsea took Maud to shop for her wedding gown. She chose a simple white gown with lace at the neckline and wrists. It was ankle length, with a short train.

Chelsea took a guess at Maud's ring size, so Josh took Stan to a jewelers to pick out the rings. He chose a simple gold ring for himself, but, for Maud he chose a gold band with a diamond in the center and two smaller diamonds on each side of the center stone.

Wedding day had arrived, it was beautifully sunny, and Josh had rented a canopy to keep guests from too much heat, but they could still see the wedding party. The off-duty officers, in their uniforms, escorted everyone to their seats and then stood at attention at the rows of seats.

Bridesmaid Chelsea walked Maud to her position at the altar, and Bo, with Bella on her leash and carrying the ring pillow, stood on the opposite side of the altar.

Sheriff Barnes, in his kilt and carrying his bagpipe, marched down the aisle to a position behind the Pastor but to the side where he could be seen.

When Josh came out of the dressing room and gave the nod, the music of the bagpipe sounded through the canopy as Sheriff Barnes began playing the Wedding March.

Stan came out of the room and walked down the aisle to stand facing Maud.

Maud handed her bouquet to Chelsea and turned to face Stan.

With a smile, the pastor looked from one to the other and then opened his Bible. "Ladies and gentlemen, we are gathered here to see this couple joined in Holy Matrimony. If there is any objection, please say it now."

He said, "Stan. In the eyes of God and, with His Blessing, do you take this woman to be your lawfully wedded wife to love and cherish and to never part?"

Tears in his eyes, Stan said, "I do."

The pastor turned to Maud and said. "Maud, in the eyes of God and, with his blessing, do you take this man to be your lawfully wedded husband, to love and cherish and to never part?"

"I do."

"I now pronounce you Husband and Wife. Stan, you may kiss the Bride."

Stan took Maud in his arms and hugged and kissed her passionately.

People shouted, with joy, as they left the canopy and headed into the church. Once inside, everyone congratulated Maud and Stan and cheered as the loving couple cut the cake.

Music was turned on and Stan and Maud began dancing. Soon, everyone was dancing or snacking at the table. It was a joyful time for everyone.

Bull and Snake were beginning to get tired of waiting, but there wasn't very much they could do. They were also getting hungry and thirsty because they hadn't thought about how long it might be before they could have something to eat. The sound of people having barbecue and cake made it even worse.

But then, the music stopped, and the crowd began coming out the door. They wanted to be there to bid Stan and Maud a happy trip on their way to their honeymoon.

As the crowd came out, Snake became excited. "Our target should be coming out pretty soon." He whispered. Then, he yanked his pistol out of the holster. "There he is! I'm going to blow his head off!"

Bull grabbed the pistol and said, "You idiot! Don't you see how many cops are over there? Take one shot, and we'll both be dead or in jail, and I don't want to face either. When everybody is gone, we'll sneak back to the pickup and go back to the farm. No one will know we were here."

Snake sat down on the ground and muttered mournfully. "We're never gonna get paid. Everything we do gets screwed up!"

Bull slapped Snake on the back and said, "don't worry, we'll get paid. I have a plan. If the old man is back from his trip and wants to know where we've been, I'll tell him my friend got worse and we went to check on him.

Chapter 18

When the wedding party had exited the church, everyone was crowded around Stan and Maud, shaking hands, hugging them, and wishing them a happy honeymoon. Happy wishes had been painted on the tailgate of Stan's pickup and strings of tin cans had been tied to the bumper.

Stan helped Maud into the pickup and got into the driver's seat. Then, he started the engine and headed off with shouts and waves from the crowd as far as they could see them.

Stan headed for the highway. "About ten miles and we'll see a bridge that goes over the stream," he said. "Then, we'll turn right onto the road that goes to the cabin."

"How long will that take?" She asked.

"About five or six miles, but be sure to watch out the windows. There are all kinds of birds. You might even see some deer. You're going to love the cabin. My son built it himself. It has four bedrooms, each with its own private bath, a dining room, a kitchen and a patio at the back with a pool. You can swim, float or just relax. There's a big fireplace, in case they come up here in the winter. There are skis, snowshoes, and sleds in the garage. They like to come in the winter just to have fun in the snow. Just a mile or so from the cabin, there's a beautiful little waterfall. There are walking trails where you can see all kinds of things. I hope you like it, Love."

Maud reached over and stroked his cheek. "Darling, if there was nothing here, I would still like it because I have you beside me." Then, she gasped! "Is that the cabin?" Stan grinned and said, "It sure is." Maud stared at it as if it was a mirage. "Wow!" She said. "He built it by himself!"

The cabin was a large, two-story building of hand hew logs. A porch stretched across the front, with porch swings at each side and chairs for comfort.

"His wife and kids pitched in to help with the work. Stan said. "It has four bedrooms, with a bath in each one. The kitchen and dining room are incredible. The living room has a huge fireplace that they keep stocked with wood. They love coming here in the winter, and the kids flop down in front of the fireplace and play games. Off to the left, there are hiking trails and you can't imagine what you see along them. Well, here we are. I'll get things unloaded, and we can go inside.

When Stan opened the door, Maud's eyes popped, and her mouth dropped. She stood, looking at everything. It was like going into an incredible hotel. A long leather couch just invited you to sit down and relax. There were recliners scattered around the room, a beautiful table in the middle of the floor and huge television on the wall.

"I've never seen anything like this," Maud said. "It's incredible."

Next was the kitchen, and it had every appliance anyone could want. Maud took a good look and said, "I guess all we have to do now is go buy some groceries." Stan grinned, opened a door, and ushered her in. "Right this way, My Lady."

Maud found herself in a pantry with several shelves of canned food, jars of several kinds of jelly, and jars filled with sugar, flour, corn meal and noodles. In the corner was dog food, cat food, and cat litter. On the other wall was a huge freezer filled with all kinds of meat, frozen vegetables and at least three kinds of ice cream. There were also frozen waffles, pancakes, biscuits, and bread. "Well," Stan said, "do you think we need to go to the grocery store?" Maud burst into laughter and gave Stan a big hug.

Stan smiled and said, "Would you like to see the bedrooms?" He picked up the luggage and headed up the stairs with Maud right behind him. The first three rooms he showed her had walls painted in soft, delicate colors. There was a large, comfortable-looking bed with a hand-pieced quilt. Recliners provided relaxing seating and there were beautiful pictures on the walls and vases of silk flowers.

Maud found herself admiring each room because they looked so comfortable. Then they went to the room that would be theirs. The walls were a soft, gentle pink with a beautiful painting of trees and flowers over the head of the bed, and surprisingly, there was a picture of their wedding, in a beautiful frame, on the dresser. She picked it up and clasped it to her breast. "This is so beautiful. I wonder who took it."

"I don't know, but whoever did it is a good photographer."

Stan took her hand and led her into the bathroom. It was an incredible room, with a Garden Tub and double showers so they could each have a shower at the same time. "I've never seen anything like this before!" Maud said

"Tyler's a wealthy man, but he's also kind and generous. I've seen him buy bags of groceries for those in need and clothes and coats for the kids. He dresses as Santa, come Christmas and hands out toys and candy to all the children. He had it tough as a kid and he likes to make things good for others. He saw an old log cabin and decided that was what he wanted, so he and Julia and the kids got to work and built it. The boys are as proud of it as he and Julia are. Now, there's one more door." He opened it and they stepped out on a balcony with a couple of chairs where they could sit and watch the stream bubbling its way along.

Trees lined the shore across the stream. And above them could be seen distant mountain peaks. Relaxed in a chair, Maud watched the swaying of the trees and suddenly, she sat forward and pointed. "Look," she said, "it's a hawk. I love the way they fly. They seldom move their wings; they just ride the air currents. I'd like to go see the waterfall sometime tomorrow. Look down there. I see a frog on one of the branches. It's catching bugs."

Stan put his glasses on and looked down. "I see the little guy. He must be really hungry. He's sure going after those bugs. Tyler and the rest of the family will be here in a couple of days. They're back from their vacation and they want to meet you. The sun's getting ready to go and I'm a little hungry. There's ham and cheese in the refrigerator, so I think I'll make myself a sandwich. How about you?"

Maud stretched and took his arm. "I think I'd like a sandwich but with mustard on it."

"What! Who ever heard of such a thing?"

Maud chuckled and said, "You just don't know what's good. I'm going to eat my sandwich and then, take a shower and hit the sack."

"Sounds perfect, a sandwich, a shower and then bed with you snuggled up in my arms."

"Then, let's get to it," Maud said. "Having your arms around me will be the end of a perfect day."

Chapter 19

The next morning, it didn't take long for a hearty breakfast. Maud made a picnic lunch to take along just in case they were out longer than anticipated. Then they were off to see the waterfall. There were beautiful plants along the way and she decided she wanted to dig up one or two when they left for home and plant them in her yard.

By the time they reached the waterfall, she had decided on a half dozen plants she wanted to take home.

When they reached the waterfall, she was in awe at the beauty of the water as it tumbled over the edge, it sparkled, and a spray of mist reached toward them. "Is it alright to cross the bridge?" She asked.

"It's strong and Tyler keeps it in good shape. It's beautiful, on the other side. They crossed the bridge and started down the path. "Look over there," Maud whispered.

Stan looked where she pointed and saw a Doe and a fawn at the water's edge. The Doe stood looking at them and then got a drink of water and walked away, with the fawn skipping along behind her.

"They were so beautiful. I've never seen anything like them before," Maud said. "They seem so tame."

"Tyler feeds them. He doesn't let anyone hurt animals on his property."

They walked along. Admiring all the foliage and laughing at squirrels scrambling in the trees to pick nuts to eat. Wispy clouds topped the mountain peaks.

They walked until they were tired and hungry. Then, they sat on a blanket Maud had brought and ate the lunch she had packed. They weren't in a hurry, so they just sat and enjoyed the scenery. Finally, it looked like it might rain, so they headed back to the cabin.

When they got to the cabin, Maud warmed up some soup and made sandwiches. Then they sat on the couch together and watched a light rain while they ate.

"This has been a wonderful day," Maud said. "I'm so glad you brought me here." She yawned and stretched.

"Are you getting tired?" Stan asked. Maud nodded, "I've never walked so much. I think I'll get a shower and hit the sack." "I think so, too," Stan said.

Dancing arm in arm, under a hot shower, in cozy pajamas and bed. Ahhh, what a pleasure.

They snuggled together, her head on his arm, her cheek against his chest. He stroked her hair and kissed her softly. Then he took a deep breath and said, "I should have told you about my past before I asked you to marry me. I'd been married before. I was in my early twenties when I fell in love with Jessica. We got married before and two years later, she got pregnant and had Tyler. Three years later, she had Casey. Then, she developed cancer and died. I had to hire someone to take care of them until I got off work. I drove a trash truck. It was a joy working with my kids. When they got old enough to go to school, I would help them with their homework. Tyler loved working with numbers, and as he grew, he mowed lawns and did odd jobs for people. He put every cent into a checking account. He thought throwing your money away on cigarettes, drugs and booze was stupid. Between what we had saved and what he had earned, we got him through college. After he graduated, he got a job with a realtor and worked his way up until he bought the company. Then he made a few investments that are really producing. That's how he earned enough to build this cabin. He met Denise two years ago, and they got married. She's pregnant, so you're gonna be a grandma."

"With Casey, it was sports. He played baseball in high school and college. He graduates this year and has two pro teams wanting him. I'm not sure which one he's going to choose. He loves baseball and he's really good at it."

"Is your family coming," Maud asked, "I'd like to meet them."

'Yes. When they heard we were getting married, they decided to take a short vacation and then come see us. They can only stay a couple of days. They should be here sometime Friday evening after Tyler closes the shop.

You know, the first time I went to the B&B, I couldn't take my eyes off you. I saw you were beautiful and treated people kindly. I didn't get to come in often because I worked late, but I came as often as I could.

Do you remember the night you had a bunch of people in? Because of the bad weather, Josh played his guitar, and I played my fiddle. People were laughing and dancing, and I got a chance to dance with you. Holding you in my arms was the most wonderful thing I ever felt."

Maud snuggled a little closer and said, "I felt like I was in Heaven. I had danced a few times before but never felt so wonderful. When you put your arms around me, I felt shivers run down my spine."

They pulled the blankets up and drifted into a peaceful sleep. The next morning, Maud was just getting ready to make breakfast when Stan asked if she would take a walk on one of the trails. She smiled and instead of breakfast, she fixed a picnic basket. "I fixed enough for breakfast and lunch."

Stan grinned and went out to the shed. He came back, pulling a wagon. "Some of the trails are bumpy, so we always keep this wagon, just in case it was a little rough. I'll put in a blanket, so we can sit on the ground if we want to."

They spread out the blanket in the shade of the trees and then sat down at the top of the hill. Maud leaned back against a tree trunk and looked up at the sky. "It's so peaceful here. The birds are singing, and you can see the tips of the mountains over the treetops. There's a hawk. They 'so graceful. Oh, look, down in the valley!"

Stan looked and saw several Does grazing the tall grass, with fawns romping along behind them. The Fawns skipped and romped like small children. After a little play time, they went to the Does to nurse. After a good feed, it was back to playtime. The little ones ran and jumped and butted heads to see who could outdo the others.

Stan and Maud laughed at their silly antics. Then, Momma and the babies turned around and disappeared into the trees. "That was fun," Maud said.

It was lunchtime, so they dug into the picnic basket and had a good meal. Then, they threw scraps to the squirrels and rabbits and birds. Then, they relaxed on the blanket and had a short snooze. When they woke up, they saw a couple of squirrels standing close to them, looking at them as if wondering what kind of creatures they were. When they moved, the squirrels took off like a shot. They walked down the hill to the cabin. The rest of the day was spent cuddling on the couch and just talking and relaxing.

The next morning, Maud was just getting ready to start breakfast when they heard a car come in the yard. Stan went to the window and shouted, "They're here!" He ran outside just as a man, a woman and a young man got out of the car. The two men got out the luggage, and the woman went toward the cabin. The older man grinned and ran toward Stan, arms held wide and a look of joy.

"Dad!" the older man shouted as he ran up and gave Stan a hug. "It's so good to see you. I've missed you." Casey graduates in a couple of months and he'll be playing pro baseball. Stan hugged Casey and said, "You have really grown, and now you're going to play pro baseball. We'll try to get down to see you play. I'm really proud of you." He hugged Casey and then turned back to Tyler and gave him another hug.

"Son, you don't know how much I've missed you. I wish we could get together more often."

Maud came up to them and handed out her hand. Tyler shook it and pulled her in for a hug. "Dad," he said. "You always had an eye for a pretty woman. That's why you married Mom. This must be Maud."

"You're absolutely right. This is Maud, the love of my life."

"Maud, would you mind if I took Dad off for a short walk? It seems like I haven't had a chance to just talk to him in forever."

"I was just getting ready to start breakfast, so you should have plenty of time to talk."

Stan and Tyler walked down toward the stream and stood watching the water go by. "Dad, Maud is an attractive woman, and I can see you care for her."

Stan nodded and said, 'I've known her for a long time but was too chicken to tell her. She's a lot like you. She helps people when they need it and, on holidays like Easter, Christmas giving and Christmas, she cooks a huge meal, and anyone who wants to come is welcome. We had a bad spring storm this year, and she brought in people who lived in poverty or lived on the street and took care of them. There are people who live in this town who worship the ground she walks on. Some of the ones, who lived on the street, have gone on to get jobs because of her."

"Dad, I'm glad you found a woman like her. I can see in her eyes how much she cares for you,"

"When I thought she might get killed, I knew I had to tell her. I couldn't stand the thought of losing her."

"What are you talking about, Dad?"

"There are two hired killers out to shoot Josh and, maybe, even Chelsea. Josh was putting a sheet of metal on the back porch, but they started shooting before he finished. Maud and I grabbed a couple of rifles and started shooting back, but one of their shots ricocheted off the metal and made a crease across her upper left arm. That's when I decided I had to tell her I loved her and asked her to marry me."

"Dad, why don't you and Maud come live with us, so we can keep you safe. Denise and I would be happy to have you with us."

"Thanks for the invitation, but Maud has her business, and she likes it. Truth be told, I like it too. I like meeting and talking to customers, and I help Bo with his dogs. You should come out some winter and let him take you on a winter camping trip. The way your bunch likes getting out in the snow, I think you'd get a kick out of it."

They were laughing and chatting when Denise yelled, "Hey, you two, breakfast is ready. You better get in here before these two hungry runts decide to eat it all."

"Guess we'd better get a move on before those two kids of ours eat everything on the table." They hurried into the kitchen and settled down for a delicious breakfast. After everything was cleaned up, they got ready for a hike and took the fishing gear along, just in case they caught something. They also took a picnic basket because someone, especially Casey, might get hungry. Young men have a tendency to want something to eat rather frequently.

It was a beautiful, sunny day, and everyone seemed to be enjoying it. Now and then, they'd sit down just to enjoy the beauty around them. The birds were singing, and they heard a turkey calling.

Maud turned to Denise and said, "Am I mistaken, or do I see a bit of a bump?"

"You're not mistaken. In about three months, Stan is going to be a grandpa and you'll be a grandma. I can hardly wait. I feel the baby moving around, and I get excited."

"Has the doctor told you what it's going to be?"

"He's saying probably another boy, but I don't care what it is. Have you ever had a child?"

Maud sighed and said, I never got married and the only boys have been the ones that worked for me, but sometimes, I felt as if they were mine. Chelsea's brother Bo has always seemed as if he was my son. He treats me as if I was his Mother. His sister treats me as if I were her Mother and now, she's married. Even the neighborhood kids treat me that way. They're always bringing me little things they've made, and the girls bring their dolls to play and want me to hold them and sing lullabies to them. If a parent wants to know where their little one is, they check with me. I knew someone who didn't have any family. When we met, we became best friends. She owned the Bed and Breakfast and when we weren't busy sometimes, we would sit on the back steps and watch the ducks swimming in the stream, with the ducklings paddling along behind. When she passed away, she willed the place to me. I've been here a long time and made a lot of friends. Those men of ours aren't doing anything. We brought fishing gear and I think we should go down to the stream and show them how to catch fish.

Denise gave a grin and started gathering up the gear. They sat on the bank and baited their hooks. "Hope I get this right. I've never been fishing before, not even at the stream behind the B@B. Maud said."

They sat in eager anticipation. Suddenly, Maud squealed and began struggling.

Denise jumped up and looked over her shoulder. Then she screamed, "You got one! You got one! Try to haul it in."

The guys heard the screams and jumped up, afraid something was wrong. They ran over and saw Denise and Maud were sitting on the stream bank.

"What's wrong? Did one of you get hurt?" Tyler asked frantically. Then, he saw Maud tugging on a fishing pole. Then he got excited. "You got one and it looks like a good one. Casey, go get the gear. We might get enough to have a fish fry. Congratulations, Maud. You got the first catch of the day. I knew this was going to be a great day."

Casey came back carrying a bucket and fishing gear. "Here you are, Tyler. I'll go a little further downstream and see if I can catch anything."

Stan set the bucket on a circle of rocks and began gathering up twigs and sticks to build a fire in case they caught enough to have a fish fry. Before long, he was skinning, gutting and cutting fish after fish. "We can cook them on a stick, but it sure would be good if we had some oil, salt, flour, and a skillet. Then we could have fried fish. There's nothing better than fried fish."

Denise got into the bag she had carried and hauled out a skillet. "How's this, Stan? I've got everything else, just in case we were lucky."

"Well, I'll be doggy! That girl thought of everything! How'd you end up with such a smart woman, Son? I think Denise and Maud are the smartest women I have heard tell of."

"Dad, when it comes to fishing, you never have to worry about having everything you need. Denise loves to fish."

Stan got a fire going and Denise got the fish on to cook and took everything out of the picnic basket. The men spread out a couple of blankets and sat down to watch the women cook lunch. There was a lot of laughter and teasing.

"After building that incredible house, don't you live in it?" Stan asked. "I can't imagine it just sitting there."

"We do live in it, Dad. We had just left to take a vacation when we heard you were getting married, so we decided to offer it to you for your honeymoon. We figured we'd be back in time to see you, and ta da here we are. I know you like this place and figured Maud would, too. I have an important meeting tomorrow, so I'll have to leave in the morning, but Denise and Casey can stay if they want to."

Denise put her hand on Tyler's shoulder and said, "I'd like to see where Maud lives. She's part of the family now. You could pick me up there. "Casey," "yes, Mom," "your Dad has a meeting tomorrow and he'll be leaving in the morning. If it's alright with Maud and Stan, I'd like to see where they live, and they could bring me back here, or I could stay there and your Dad could pick me up. Do you want to go with him or go with me"

Casey thought for a minute and spoke to Maud. "What did you say the name of the guy with the dogs is?"

"His name is Bo." Maud said.

He grinned from ear to ear and said. "I want to go with you. Mom. I want to see the dogs. You know how I like dogs."

Denise laughed and patted his shoulder. "When you get a dog, what are you going to do with it when you have a Pro Baseball game?"

"I'll take it with me. I'll put it on the seats, on a leash, and I know the guys will take care of it for me. I think the coach would let me do that, but if he won't, I'll hire a dog sitter. The Cardinals and Yankees want me and I'm thinking of going with the Yankees. I plan to get an apartment that allows pets and I have a friend who would share the apartment and he could take care of my dog when I'm away for a game. You know Billy Barrister, Mom. He's as nuts about dogs as I am."

Denise laughed and gave him a hug. "You could always bring it to the house and we'd take care of it for you. What kind of dog do you want?"

"I really don't really know. I think I'll check out Bo's dogs and get his advice."

Maud patted his shoulder and said. "We can have supper and a good rest. Then, in the morning, we'll leave about the time Tyler does. That way, you can tell him goodbye and to be careful. Then we can pile up in the car and head for the Bed and Breakfast."

Chapter 20

As they went down the road, Denise said, "This reminds me so much of when I was a kid. We lived in the country and when I see the farmhouses and the livestock, I remember Daddy on the tractor feeding or plowing to sow what he was going to plant. *When I got a little older, he'd let me drive the tractor. My job was to feed the chickens, and I loved it when they came running. Knowing they were going to be fed. I also harvested eggs. Momma taught me how to cook and bake, and I learned how to take care of the house.* I think that's why I like the cabin so much. *It reminds me of home.*

"We're pretty countrified around here, Maud said. People are friendly, and I get quite a few repeat customers. Some of the truckers stop by for breakfast and, then, after they get off work. I've made quite a few friends that way. Now, I have even more friends with your family, except you're more my family than my friends. Hope I see you more often, especially when Casey starts playing Pro Baseball. He and Bo will probably become good friends since Bo likes baseball and Casey likes dogs."

Would you mind if I look around?

"Help yourself." Maud said. "Bedrooms and baths are down the hall, and there's a back porch where you can relax and watch the ducks and their little ones. I'll make some lunch and we can eat out at the Side Porch Café. Since it's Sunday, there won't be any customers and we can just sit and watch the world go by. Josh, Chelsea and Bo will be back from church, and they can join us. I fixed enough for everybody. By the way, where is Stan?"

"*He went home to get his fiddle. He thought we might like a little music, and Casey is down admiring the dogs. The bedrooms are beautiful. Did you make the quilts?*"

"*No, ladies at the church, keep me supplied.* When visitors see the quilts, they often order one, which makes good income for our church ladies. Some of them don't have much money, so we give them pieces of material to work with. They are so talented. Several of us have been thinking about opening a little shop for them. Chelsea will probably be there, she's learning to quilt."

"*That sounds wonderful.*" Denise said. "I'd like to order four of them. They would be perfect for the bedrooms in the cabin."

"*If you'd like to meet some of the ladies after lunch, we can go down to the church and they can show you some patterns and materials and you'll get a chance to meet Chelsea. She's Josh's wife.*"

"Oh, yes, yes. I'd love that."

"When the men get back from whatever they're doing, Bo can take Casey down to see the dogs."

Denise smiled. "He's wanted a dog for quite a while. When he and his friend, Gavin, get moved into their apartment, he can have one. The apartments are pet friendly, and his buddy can take care of the dog when he's at a game. Gavin loves dogs as much as he does."

"Well," Maud said. "The guys are here. Denise, the big, good-looking one is Josh. He's Chelsea's husband, and the other one is Bo and I know Casey wants to talk to him. Don't you, Casey?"

"You're the one with the dogs!" Casey said. "I was looking at them through the fence. They're incredible!"

"Would you like to go down and be introduced to them?"

"I'd like nothing better."

They went down the back steps and Bo unlocked the gate. "Rusty." He called and a beautiful black and brown dog came to him, "This is Rusty. He's my lead dog." He gave a short whistle and a slightly smaller dog came to him. "This is Bella. She's my second. They keep the team in line. Each dog has a name and they all know their commands. It's like when I give Rusty a command, "Sit." Rusty sat and didn't move. "Down," Rusty lay down on his belly, "Stay" Rusty didn't move a muscle. He just stared intently at Bo, "Come" Rusty immediately came to him.

This is a small town, and we have a small police force. With all the trees, cliffs, and other kinds of danger, people who aren't familiar with them get lost or hurt, and we don't have enough people to safely find them. That's why I decided to have Rusty trained to find people, and Bella is trained for Search and Rescue. There are a few others having their dogs trained so we can help the police department when they need us."

"Wow! Casey said. I've heard of dogs doing that but never thought I'd see one.

"Would you like to see how Rusty works?" Bo asked.

Casey grinned and said, "Sure would."

"Give me your jacket and go over the bridge across the stream. Then, find a real secure hiding place in the trees. Make sure he can't see you."

Casey took off at a dead run and disappeared into the trees. Bo gave him several minutes to hide, and then Bo let Rusty smell the jacket and said, "Seek." Rusty sniffed the jacket and the ground. Then he raised his head and smelled the air. Without any kind of command, he streaked across the bridge and into the trees.

Bo could hear the sound of him searching through the trees and brush. In about ten minutes, he heard a bark. He grinned and followed the sound. The bark got louder and he saw Casey standing with his back to a tree and Rusty on guard. "O.K Rusty. Good job." He called the dog to him and gave him a good patting and praise. "Can I come out now?" Casey asked. "Sure, Rusty knows we were just practicing."

Casey brushed leaves and twigs off his shirt. "I had so much stuff covering me. I thought he'd never find me. How did he do it?"

"Dogs have a better sense of smell than people. I let him smell your jacket and he followed your scent trail right to you."

"I can't wait to get a dog, but I don't know what kind or how to train it."

Bo thought for a minute and said, "I have an idea, but I'll have to run it by your Sister-in-law first."

They ran up the stairs and Casey couldn't wait to tell Denise what they had done. She thanked Bo for his kindness to Casey and then Bo said, "We have an animal shelter here, and, with your approval, I'd take Casey down there so he could see different kinds of dogs. It might help him decide what he wants.

Denise hugged Bo and said, "I think it's a wonderful idea. I'm sure Tyler would approve, also.

The two young men dashed out the door, jumped into Bo's car and were on their way. Since the shelter was open seven days a week, twenty-four hours a day, they had no problem going in and being escorted into the dog area. Casey stared longingly at every dog. Sometimes, he knelt and stuck his fingers through the wire. Some of them came to lick his fingers and then went to the back of their cages.

A brown and black dog that was a little bigger than Bella licked his fingers and stared up into his face.

As they walked down the corridor, the dog watched their every step and uttered a faint whimper. Casey had a strange feeling and when he looked over his shoulder, the dog was still staring at them. As they started to leave, it whimpered and gave a little bark. Casey turned around and went back to kneel in front of the dog. They stared into each other's eyes, and it put its paws up on the wire and whimpered as if it was pleading for him to take it. Casey turned to the caretaker and asked, "Does this one belong to anyone?" "No. He's been here for about three months, and I've never seen him act like this. He's a nice little fellow, but he seems so sad. I think he'd make someone a great pet."

Casey knelt, staring into the dog's eyes. "I want him. He needs someone to love him."

"Are you sure your folks want you to get a dog right now?" Bo asked.

"Well, I'm an adult. I'll graduate from the University in less than two months and Gavin and I will be moving into our pet-friendly apartment. A month or so after that, I'll be playing Major League Baseball. So, I think I should be free to make up my own mind and I want this dog. Since he's going to be my pal, I think I'll name him Buddy. When the cage was opened, the dog jumped into his arms and laid its head under Casey's chin. Casey smiled and hugged the dog as he carried him to the front desk. "All I have to do is get him trained," he said.

"You shouldn't have too much trouble with that." The caretaker said. "He belonged to Harry Bixby, who had taught him how to take care of his sheep. One of the neighbors saw Harry lying in the field and went to check on him. Harry was dead; he'd had a heart attack. He didn't have a family, so they brought the dog to the shelter. We're a No Kill Shelter and he's been here three years. I've been hoping someone would adopt him. He'll be a good pet for you. I don't know where you're from, but there should be a trainer you can depend on. Here's his collar and leash and he's had all his shots. Keep in touch; I'd like to know how he does. My name's Jake Johnson. Here's my card."

Casey put the collar on Buddy, **attached the leash and led him to the car with Buddy walking right beside him.**

With a big smile, Jake watched as the dog walked along, looking up at Casey. "Good luck, fellow. You finally got someone who wants you." Jake said.

Casey put Buddy in the back seat and said, "Stay." He stretched out and, with a deep, contented sigh, went to sleep.

When they got back to the Bed and Breakfast, Casey took Buddy out of the car and they went inside. Denise and Maud came out of the kitchen and came to a stop when they saw Casey leading a dog.

"I thought you went to look at dogs. I didn't know you were going to bring one home," Denise said. "Are you going to keep him?"

"His name's Buddy and I am going to keep him. He's a sweet-tempered, gentle dog. If you had seen the way he kept looking at me, you wouldn't wonder why I wanted him."

Denise walked up to Buddy and held out her hand. He gave her hand a look and gazed up at her. She stroked his head and said, "he seems like a great dog and I'm glad you got what you wanted. I know Tyler's going to approve of him."

Maud knelled in front of Buddy and said. "Take care of your pal. I know he'll take good care of you. Bo, what kind of dog is he?"

"From his size and coloring, I'd say he's probably a German shepherd, collie mix. They're both gentle and easy to train. I'd say Casey got himself a good dog. That mix is very good about keeping its master safe and obeying commands."

"Tyler should be here soon," Denise said. "I'm anxious for him to meet Buddy. And Maud, thank you for taking me to see the quilting. They said they would ship the quilts to me as soon as they're finished. I know they're going to be perfect for the cabin."

They had just sat down for supper when Tyler walked in the door.

"I hope you haven't finished off everything. I'm starving." Denise walked up to him, patted his cheek, and said, "A-w-w, poor Tyler. I'll bet he hasn't had a bite all day except a big steak with a baked potato and a slice of apple pie."

Maud laughed and went into the kitchen. Then she returned with a ham and cheese sandwich, potato salad and a big bowl of ice cream, with caramel sauce and a cherry, on top. "Here you go. She said, you eat it all up, so you won't get skinny."

Everyone laughed as he gobbled it down. "That was good, he said. Better than any old steak. What's been going on today?"

Denise grinned and pointed. "Turn around and you'll see."

Tyler turned around and his mouth gapped open. "What in the world! Where did that dog come from? It isn't one of yours, is it, Bo?"

Casey led the dog over to Tyler and said. "He's mine. I got him at the pet shelter." "He's a beautiful dog." Tyler said. "What breed is he?" "He's probably a German Shepard, Collie mix. He's very gentle and obedient. When we get home, I want to find a good trainer for him."

Tyler sat back on his heels and got a good face washing from a very wet tongue. He laughed and wiped the kisses off his face. "He's a beautiful dog," Tyler said. "Have you told Marty that you have a dog?"

"Not yet. I want to surprise him when we get home."

Everyone was around Casey and Buddy, hugging and petting, when Stan walked in, carrying his fiddle. "Hey! What's going on here?" Maud stood up, gave him a kiss, and said, "Casey got a dog."

"A dog! Where is it?"

The crowd parted and Stan gave a big grin. "Now, that is a fine-looking dog. Where did you get him?"

"I got him at the pet shelter. We took to each other right away."

Stan shook his head. "I never thought I'd see this fine fellow at the pet shelter. What kind is he?"

"German Shepard and Collie mix."

"I've heard of that mix, and they're really dependable animals." He squatted and stroked Buddy's neck. You take really good care of that young fellow, okay? After dinner, I thought you all might like a little music, so I went and got my fiddle. How about you, Josh? Do you feel like a little music?"

"Sounds good."

When supper was cleaned up, out came the guitar and fiddle and the music was on. There was clapping and singing and the ladies were dancing. Even Buddy got into the act. He pranced around and let out an occasional bark. Chelsea picked up his front feet and danced him around. He looked into her face and gave her a good lick.

They were playing some country songs when, suddenly, Casey pulled a harmonica out of his pocket and joined in. The rest of the music stopped when they heard Casey playing with the rest of the music. Everyone was astonished because they didn't know he could play the harmonica. Tyler walked over and gave him a big hug. "When did you learn to play that thing," he asked?

Casey grinned and said, "I've been working at it for about six months. I wanted to get good at it before I let anybody know.

Gavin and I have been performing at the nursing home down the street. The people really seem to enjoy it."

Tyler shook his head and said, "Casey, Casey, you've given me more surprises than I could ever imagine. You're a grade-A student, you're going to be a professional baseball player, you got yourself a dog and now, I know you can play the harmonica. What else are you planning?"

"Oh, I don't know. I may decide to become an astronaut and walk on the moon or maybe dive to the bottom of the sea."

Tyler shook his head and said, "I wouldn't put it past you. Ever since you were a kid, you've planned things and then did them. Josh, would you believe it, when he was seven years old, he built a fruit drink stand and ended up making over five hundred dollars. He put it in a savings account and did odd jobs until he had enough money to start college. I am one proud big brother. It wouldn't surprise me if he didn't become President of the United States someday." He gave Casey a big hug.

"Nah, politics is too boring," Casey said. "I think I'll buy an airplane and learn to fly. I could get from one game to another faster that way."

Tyler just shook his head and gave his brother a slap on the back. I've had a busy day, so I think I'll hit the sack. How about you, Honey?"

Denise yawned and, after bidding everyone good night, headed for the bedroom. Tyler followed and after a tender hug and kiss, took a shower, got into his pajamas and crawled into bed. He snuggled up to her and said, "I'm glad Casey got to know such decent people. We're going to keep in touch with them. He and Marty are going to love having that dog around.

The next morning, with breakfast over and the dishes done, it was time to say goodbye. Casey loaded the luggage and went inside to tell Bo goodbye. There was plenty of hugging and wishes for safety on the way home. Tyler hugged Maud and shook Stan's hand.

"It's been a pleasure getting to know all of you. Tyler said. Stan told me about the danger you've been in. Be careful. We wouldn't want anything to happen to you."

They climbed in the car and, with a wave, took off down the road. "It's 'beautiful here," Denise said, "I'd like to take another visit."

"As soon as I can get some more time off, we'll make a trip back, Tyler said. Casey, how's Marty doing? "

"He's walking on crutches and his boss has him doing his work from home. Of course, with a brain like his, he can finish his work in three or four hours. I'll be glad when we get home so I can walk in the door with Buddy beside me. He's gonna freak. I just hope he doesn't try to jump up and walk across the floor without his crutches. He's wanted a dog ever since I first met him. His girlfriend is just as bad as he is. Every dog she sees, she wants to pet it."

"Does she know someone who's a dog trainer?

"Tyler, that's what she does. She trains police dogs, seeing eye dogs, trackers, search and rescue. If a dog needs training, she can do it. I can hardly wait until Gavin and Missy get to see Buddy".

Tyler left Casey at the apartment and then headed home. Gavin was watching TV but, when Casey walked through the door with Buddy beside him, Marty's eyes got big, and his mouth dropped open. "You've got a dog!" he exclaimed. Casey took Buddy and introduced him. His tail wagged and he licked Marty's hand. "He's beautiful, but where did you get him? "The town where we were, has a No-Kill-Shelter and Bo took me there." "And who is Bo?"

Casey waved good-bye to Tyler and then sat down. Buddy climbed in the seat and snuggled with his head on Casey's leg. "Where were you?"

"You were at the wedding, the man walking with a cane is Josh, the woman beside him is his wife, Chelsea and Bo is her brother. He took me to the shelter and while we were walking down the corridor looking at the dogs, I got an odd feeling. When I looked over my shoulder, Buddy was staring at me. Every step I took, he watched me. When we started to leave, he whined and gave a sad little bark. I went back to his cage and he pawed at it. I knew he needed someone to love him, so I adopted him. He's a good dog. He's obedient and I want to get him trained.."

"I want to get him trained, and I know Nancy could do it. Do you think she would have time?"

Just then, Nancy walked in carrying a large pizza. "Hi. Guys. I brought us a pizza for supper. Hey! Whose dog is that?" Gavin told her the whole story and she walked over to Buddy, hugged him, and got a slurpy kiss in return. She laughed and said, "I think you're just a big lover." She turned to Casey and asked, "Are you planning to get him trained?"

"Yes, I do. When I start playing baseball, Marty will be taking care of him for me and I want him to be obedient. Sometimes, I may take him with me and put him on a leash and fasten it to the equipment post."

Nancy petted Buddy and looked at Casey. "After work, I'll help you get him trained. I don't think I'll have any problem with him at all. He looks like a German Shepard, Collie mix, so he will not only train well but he will be very protective of you both.

Every night, Nancy came and worked with Buddy. Casey took him to the fenced backyard so he could romp around and clean up after him when he needed to do a job. When he was at his classes, Marty would take over. He would bark in the yard but never in the apartment. If he needed to go to the yard, he would go to Gavin, put his paw on Gavin's knee and give a little bark. Then he would go to the door and wait for Marty to take him to the yard. Then Casey would take Buddy for a walk to the dog park, where he made friends with other dogs while Casey sat under a tree and watched.

Chapter 21

After some play, he walked him home and talked to him, and Buddy would listen intently as if he understood every word Casey said. He waved at neighbors and Buddy gave them a friendly bark and wagged his tail at them.

By the time they got home, Marty had supper ready and Casey cleaned up the kitchen so they could all relax.

"Why don't you get your scooter out and come to the park with us?" Casey said, "You'd get a kick out of watching Buddy play with the other dogs. Then we could go to Mr. Chang's and have something to eat."

Marty thought about it and grinned. "How about tomorrow? The weather is supposed to be nice and I haven't had anything at Mr. Chang's in a long time. It's no fun when you go by yourself."

When Casey got home, Marty was ready to go. He laughed and laughed at the dogs as they romped and chased each other. Then, they headed for the restaurant. Mr. Chang came out, drying his hands. "Well, look who comes see me! Mr. Chang looked at Marty and said, "I know you have an accident. Don't get out much, but a pretty young lady came to take food home for you. She knows just what you like. She likes you very much. You maybe marry her?" Marty gave an embarrassed grin and said, "When my leg heals, I plan to propose to her. Tell me when the wedding is going to happen and I make you a big wedding dinner. Then, he looked at Casey. "You graduate soon, and I find out you going to be a professional baseball player. Which team you choose?"

"I've signed a contract with the Yankees, Casey said. "Mr. Chang jumped in the air. "Yankees, my favorite team. I go many times this last season. When school, here have game, and you play, I go watch. You very good! I think you be big success when you start with Yankees. You no order. I make you both best meal, on menu. I bring nice dog something good, too." He gave them a wave and headed inside. "There come pretty girl. She eat with you, too." He said. Nancy waved at him and sat down. "I didn't expect to see you here. I was going to bring something for supper. I'm happy to see you out of the apartment. What brought you out??

"Casey takes Buddy to the dog park and he talked me into going with him. It was fun, watching the dogs romp. Buddy has made a couple of friends."

When Mr. Chang came back with a piled platter of food, he set it down and made a slight bow to Nancy. "She nice young lady. You take good care of her. I be glad when baseball start. I miss when can't see. You need anything else, just let me know."

Casey smiled and said, "When I start playing, I'll get you a season ticket so you can come to the games when you want, free."

Mr. Chang clapped his hands and danced a little jig. "You bet I come every time I can.

Casey dived into the tray, enjoying every bite. "Mr. Chang is a good guy. He treats everyone like family.

After they had finished their meal, they headed home, and Nancy gave Buddy a few lessons. "He's a smart dog. He's learning fast. He and you will take good care of each other when Casey can't be here. You know, when you get so you can take short walks, you can put him on a leash and he'll take care of you. I can hardly wait until that happens. Well, I'd better get to my job." She gave him a kiss and headed out the door.

"I've never been to the Bed and Breakfast, Gavin said. I'd like to get to know everyone and see Bo's dogs. I can't even imagine owning a team of snow dogs."

"Tell you what," Casey said, "this weekend, after class, I'll take you out there and you can get acquainted but be very careful. There are a couple of guys who have been trying to kill Josh. The Sheriff found out that they are a couple of hired killers."

"What! Hired killers! Tell me what's been happening!"

"I heard Maud and Stan and Tyler talking about it. Two guys, wearing dark clothes were sneaking toward the house. Bo had left the dogs out of their kennels, and they saw the guys and started barking. Bo opened the gate and the dogs started after the intruders. Rusty attacked the tall man, tearing part of his pant leg and ripping his shirt. There's a stream behind the house with ducks, and Josh and Chelsea took a walk down there to feed the ducks leftover bread. Josh walked with a heavy walking stick because he'd been in an accident. They had just walked into the trees when a big, strong man attacked him. He turned and slammed that stick into the guy's ribs so hard he could hardly breathe. Josh slammed him several more times and the guy ran. The smaller guy was looking for Chelsea and he was carrying a pistol. She was in the shed, where they keep the canoes and paddles. When the guy went by the door, she brought the edge of a paddle down across his wrist, knocking the gun out of his hand and kicked it into the water, then she smashed him across the face, breaking his nose and beating him with that paddle. Josh said he was screaming and rolling around, trying to keep her from hitting him. Josh said the guy took off like a ruptured duck, screaming until he disappeared into the trees.

The funniest thing that happened was when Josh and Stan were putting up a sheet of metal on the Climbing Rock side of the back porch. Josh saw a bright flash of light from the Rocks, so he pushed Chelsea down and covered her with his body. Then, shooting started. Maud and Stan grabbed a couple of rifles from the gun locker and started shooting. Maud is a really good shot. The short guy tumbled partway down the rocks and the big guy had to grab him and pull him back up. Josh said nobody knows if they hit him or if he was just clumsy. The shooting from the rocks pinged against the metal, but one ricocheted and hit Maud across the upper arm. It wasn't bad, just like a scratch. When Stan saw it, he went nuts. He wanted to take her to the hospital, but Chelsea looked at it and told him it was just a scratch and she would clean it and put a band-aid on it.

"No, no! She's hurt. I love her and I want to marry her."

Casey said, "I heard Josh say Stan thought he was too old and not good enough for her, but he's been in love with her since he first met her. That's why he came over so often. He just wanted to see her."

Maud went to him and gave him a kiss. *"I love you too."* She said.

"Why didn't you say anything?" he asked.

"Because the guy is supposed to do the proposing, not the woman." She said.

It was funny to see him jumping around. "She loves me. She loves me!" he said and then he grabbed her and started kissing her. "She loves me and I didn't know it."

Everyone was jumping around and shouting, "You should have seen it. I was having so much fun. I wore myself out. We were all happy for Maud and Stan."

"But why would anyone want to kill them?" Marty asked, 'They're good people."

"I don't know," Casey said, "but I heard the man who hired those guys were drunk and caused an accident t that killed Josh's wife and his unborn baby, and he was hurt pretty bad. The guy was arrested and put in jail, but he got out somehow. I think that guy's trying to get revenge for being put in jail. I've read about guys like that and they try to get back at the person they hurt. They blame the other person and try to get even if there's no sense to it. They're all more than a little crazy, so they want to get even.

Guess we'd better head home. Nancy will be there soon with something for supper and to work with Buddy. The evening was a time for watching TV and relaxing. Then Casey thought of something. "I have an idea, and I think both you and Nancy would like it. I'll ask her when she gets here.."

Classes are out for two weeks, Casey said. "How about taking a trip around the state and take in the sights? Colorado is a beautiful state and there's a lot to see. Up near Grand Junction, there's a place they call BOOK CLIFF because the ocean was once that deep and there are images of all kinds of sea creatures imbedded in the rock. I could park close enough for you to see them. We could go to Denver and Rocky Mountain Park. It's the top tourist attraction in Colorado. Then, there's Pikes Peak and they dug a tunnel through one of the mountains, so you don't have to drive up it. When I was a kid, I usually spent part of the summer with my grandparents. Sometimes, we'd pile into the car just to take a ride. Grandma loved asparagus and along the irrigation ditches, she'd find sacks of them. There was also a small lake with a ramp where you could park. A lot of guys went there to fish. One day, a guy wearing the waders that come up over your chest and have straps. He was out in the water and caught a really big fish. He got tangled up in his fishing gear and that fish pulled him all over that lake. He was screaming and yelling for help. He couldn't have gotten hurt because the waders were holding him. Finally, he got close enough that two other guys grabbed him and pulled him in. It was so funny we laughed all the way home. What do you think? We could spend a couple of weeks just enjoying ourselves. We could take Buddy and Nancy could come if she wanted to.

Just then, Nancy walked in with hamburgers, fries and soft drinks. Casey helped set things out and said, "Nancy, I have an idea I've talked about with Marty and want to talk to you about it. He told her about the trip, all the places they'd go, and the things they'd see. Marty's' all for it, and we thought you'd like to go along with us. Would your boss let you have some time off?" Marty started laughing. "I'd love a trip like that. I've been in this apartment so long; I'm going stir-crazy.

"Sounds great and I don't have to ask the boss. I am the boss. I learned about dog training and started my own business. Unless I have a customer, I can take off any time I want. When do you want to leave?

"My brother, Tyler, has a great motor home and I know he'd let us use it. It has living quarters, with a TV, a kitchen with a table and chairs and three small bedrooms. Hold on and I'll call him. He says yes and he and Denise will stock the shelves and refrigerator. Pots and pans and linens are already in it and they'll drop it off tomorrow morning. So. Get your stuff ready and if you like to fish, bring your gear. This is going to be a lot of fun.

The next morning, after Tyler and Denise delivered the motor home, Casey, Nancy, and Marty were ready to go. They helped

Marty get inside and seated. They put Buddy in and, with a lot of laughter and waving, got started on their exciting trip. Denise put her hand over her mouth and said, "I hope they'll be careful."

Tyler took her in his arms and hugged her. "Honey, they're three careful young people and I know they will be very careful. I told Casey to call when they got settled for the night. Don't worry."

As they traveled down the road, Nancy's head was constantly on the move. Every time she saw something new, like turkeys or a herd of horses or cows, especially if there were calves. She squealed and pointed. She was raised on a farm and she loved seeing the livestock. She gave a little sigh and said, "Sometimes I wish I was still on our old farm. I loved taking care of the animals. Dad had riding gear and he would let me ride his favorite horse. I really miss living in the country. It's because I love animals so much that I got into dog training. Buddy is such an easy animal to work with."

Marty turned and looked over his shoulder. "Nancy, I didn't know about you living on a farm. I did the same thing. We had cattle and I helped with the calving. You know, I was going to wait until I had gotten completely healed but I can't wait any longer. I'm in love with you and I want to marry you." She lunged forward and began kissing him. Tears ran down her cheeks and she sobbed. "Why didn't you say so before this? You don't know long I've waited to hear you ask me to marry you."

"I guess I thought you might not want a cripple and you might want to live in town. Would you like to buy a farm and have animals to take care of?

She hugged and kissed him again. I'd like nothing better. I like chickens and horses and I'd like a couple of goats. They're so much fun."

Casey couldn't help grinning as they chattered on about farming. Their eyes were sparking as they talked about it. "Well. I've never done any farming," he said. "But I'd like to visit and maybe help out once in a while. Have you thought about when you want the wedding?"

I don't think we've figured that out yet, but I want you to be my bridegroom." Finally, the merriment settled and they relaxed. "Where are we going to spend the night?" Nancy asked. "There's a trailer park just about five miles ahead," Casey said. "You can rent a space and hook up to water and electricity and even have a place to attach the toilet. There are fireplaces where you can build a fire to cook on. Some of us from the University would come down and have a real fun time. A lot of people would join us and we'd toast wieners and play music and dance. It was a lot of fun. There are probably places where you can park as we drive from place to place. I hope you bring your swim gear because several of the lakes have great swimming and boating. I see the camping place ahead. I'll pull in and reserve a place for us."

Casey drove up to the office and paid for a space where there were trees they could sit under. He and Nancy got out of the chairs and placed them around a cement cooking pit. Then they helped Gavin get out and sat in one of the chairs. Each pit had a wood pile so a fire could be built. Casey built a fire and then he and Nancy got out the food. They were just ready to roast wieners when a tall. Slender man came up, with a young boy trailing behind.

"Howdy, folks. After you eat, come over to our bus. We're planning on having a shindig. Some of the other campers will be there. One of the guys plays guitar and another plays banjo. One of the ladies has a voice like an angel. We'd welcome you to join the fun. He looked down at Gavin and said, "Bobby Joe has a wheelchair in his trailer, and he's happy to let you use it for the party. The little boy crept around the man, his eyes on Buddy. The man looked down at him and said, "Son, you know you aren't supposed to touch a dog unless the owner says it's okay."

Casey smiled and said, "Don't worry, Sir. Buddy is a very gentle dog. If your little guy wants to pet him, I have no objection. What's your name?" "I'm Jimmy and I'm five years old." "My dog's name is Buddy, and he likes people. Would it be okay if Jimmy pets Buddy?"

"My name's Ralph, my wife is Mable, the oldest is Jackson, the next is Sandy and the youngest is Jimmy and if it's okay, he wants to pet your dog, it's alright."

"Buddy is a gentle animal." Casey said "so it's all right if Jimmy and Buddy have a little play time."

The child started moving toward Buddy, but the dog beat him to it. Buddy ran to Jimmy and began covering him with slobbery doggy kisses. Jimmy laughed and went to his knees and gave Bubby a big hug. Soon, they were running all over, playing chase. Jimmy was running so hard; he could hardly breathe. He sat down on the ground and Buddy flopped over his legs. "I wike Buddy. He wots of fun. I want a dog someday. Daddy says when I'm a little bigger, I can have one, but bigger ones can get too rough. Well," Ralph said. "hope to see you at the shindig and I have a wheelchair in my vehicle, I'll bring it over so this young fella can join in," Ralph said, patting Gavin on the shoulder. He headed over to his motorhome and then returned with a wheelchair.

Casey said, "I'll get us something to eat and, then, if you want to, we'll go to the party. They quickly ate and then, Casey pushed Gavin over to where the music was going. After a couple of songs from the men and a song from one of the women,

Nancy said, "I've heard some good music, but you guys could be a band!"

Ralph laughed and said, "That's what we are. We've been taking a short vacation and in a couple of weeks, we have a two gigs to get back on. We'll be leaving in the morning and we'll be on the road again. We'll be busy until almost Christmas. Then, we'll take a short break."

Nancy sighed and said, "I'd love to come to one of your concerts."

Ralph smiled and said, "if you're anyplace near St. Louis, I'll take your names and have some tickets left for you. Be sure you see Rocky Mountain National Park. It's the most tourist destination in Colorado. The lakes are all incredibly blue, surrounded by tall mountains. I've even seen herds of deer strolling across the water. Hold on, a minute." He went in his camper and came back out carrying a map. He handed it to Tyler and said. I marked every place we went. It might help you decide where you want to go and what you want to see. Well, I think I'm ready to hit the sack. Morning comes early when you're on the road. Here's my card, with my phone number on it. If you ever find yourselves where playing, give me a call and I'll see that you get in. It was nice to meet you, folks. Hope you have a happy vacation." As they stepped into the motor home, Buddy ran up to Jimmy and they gave each other a happy goodbye. When they pulled out, Jimmy was waving, and Buddy was barking. "I really enjoyed meeting that family," Nancy said. "we'll have to watch the concert papers to see if they're close enough to take the whole family to see them." As they traveled down the highway, everything they saw amazed them, small animals digging holes. Flowering bushes, flocks of small birds filling the sky. "I'm glad we decided to take this trip." Nancy said.

It wasn't long before they saw a sign that said Rocky Mountain National Park. They turned in and went to the parking area, where they got out Gavin's chair and helped him in it. As they went around the motorhome, Nancy gasped and put her hands over her mouth. Gavin put his hand on her arm and said, "Is something wrong, Nancy? Are you okay?"

She stared over the lake and said, "I've never seen anything so beautiful?"

The lake was incredibly blue and sparkled like a gemstone. Behind it were mountains so high they seemed to reach the sky. The sun made the mountains sparkle.

Gavin suddenly said, "Look! Look over there!" He pointed to his left and when the other two looked, they saw a herd of deer wading across the end of the lake. The animals walked by as if no one was there.

"I can see what looks like trails. Why don't you two take a walk and see what you can see? I know Buddy would enjoy it."

Nancy said, "I don't want to leave you here all by yourself." "That's okay. I'll just sit and watch the birds. You know how I like watching birds. I see some hawks. I love the way they spread their wings and ride the thermals. You go on and I'll be fine. "

"Well, if you're sure. I'm going to that building and see if I can get a map. I wouldn't want us to get lost."

Gavin grinned as they headed out. Then he got out his binoculars and watched the birds. He was entranced by their grace. Then, to his surprise, he saw an eagle. Suddenly he was startled by a voice behind him. He looked and saw two men walking toward him.

"Hello, one said. We saw your friends walking toward one of the trails. We have a special program we thought you might enjoy. My brother is handicapped, and he kept wishing he could come to the park. A friend of mine had a golf cart he was going to get rid of, so I bought it. I put my brother in it and drove him all around. He was so happy; he talked a golfer friend into getting another cart. Raymond here drives one cart, and I drive the other. Sometimes we have five or six people who need rides. It isn't just handicapped we take but older people who have trouble getting around. When we saw you sitting here, we thought you might like a ride. How about it? Would you like to take a ride? You might see more than your friends will."

Gavin looked from one to the other. "You mean I could see more of the park?" "You could see a lot more." Gavin grinned with excitement. "I'd love to take a ride.

"I can push you ever where the carts are. My name is Rodney. He pushed Gavin over where the golf carts were parked. "Can you stand, or do you need a lift?" Rodney helped Gavin stand and got him in the card. Then he and Rodney climbed in the driver's seat and they were on their way,

As they headed for a trail, Rodney said, "there are more than 140 peaks in this park that rise above 11,000 feet, in altitude, including Longs Peak at 14,259 feet. We're going to take this left trail where you'll see some incredible things. Gavin's eyes were as big as dollars as he looked around. There were small animals scampering around and trees so tall he couldn't see the tops.

They came into a small clearing and Gavin said, "Look! Look! It's a beaver and it's chewing down a small tree!"

Raymond smiled and said, "Beavers are the largest aquatic animals in this country. They look for ponds or lakes that have banks above water level, then they dig holes and cut down trees they drag into the hole to build their homes. They also build dams to keep flooding out of their homes. They love water and spend a lot of time swimming. It's fascinating to see how they work. Just don't try to pet them. Their teeth could take your fingers off.

Rodney drove on down the trail and Gavin's head was constantly on the move to see everything. A couple of miles down the trail, Rodney stopped and pointed up. On a ledge over their heads, Gavin could see a nest with little heads peeping over the edge. Then, he saw an eagle land in the nest and begin feeding her little ones. "Wow!" Gavin said. "I never thought I'd see anything like this."

Everything Gavin saw was amazing. Sunshine made some rock ledges sparkle as if they were covered with gems. Deer roamed the woods, birds had nests in the trees and butterflies and dragonflies created a palate of color.

"Well," Rodney said, "I guess we'd better head back. Your friends may be wondering where you are." They headed back down the trail with Raymond pointing out things they might have missed. "Wait a minute, Raymond said." He hopped out of the cart and picked up a stone that had tumbled from a ledge. Its colors were reds and orange, with streaks of grey. "Here you are. This will remind you of where you've been if you're going to Denver. It's only 55 miles from here, and they have an incredible zoo."

Gavin caressed the stone and thanked Raymond.

Nancy and Casey were just getting back when she saw Gavin's empty chair. "That's Gavin's chair but where is he?" She was in a panic.

A man in a uniform came out of the building and said, "Don't worry, Ma'am. We have a special for folks who can't get around. We have a couple of golf carts and two young men who take those who are handicapped, or elderly on trips down some of the trails. In fact, that's probably them, coming now."

She ran up to the cart, as Rodney and Raymond helped Gavin out of it and into his chair. "Hope you had an enjoyable trip," Rodney said.

"It was specular. I've never done anything so incredible."

Nancy wiped tears from her eyes and thanked the young men. Then she took a $20 dollar bill from her purse to hand to them, but they said they didn't want her money because they enjoyed what they did. "You might have a breakdown on one of your carts and this might help fix it." Chase and Gavin took money out of their pockets and handed it to them. Chase said she's right. Someone might miss a lot of enjoyment because one of your carts was in bad shape. We want you to take this and put it to good use." "If you want to spend the night in a rest stop, just go to a service station and most of them can tell you where to go. There are a couple of good drive-ins along the way, too. Take care of yourselves and we'd like to see you again sometime."

Chase climbed into the motorhome and, with lots of Goodbyes and waving were on their way to Denver. They found a good drive-through restaurant and picked up a really good meal so Nancy wouldn't have to cook and a really great place where they could park and just relax.

The next morning, Nancy fixed breakfast and then they were on their way to the zoo. It was huge, with every animal they could imagine. They laughed at monkeys playing, stared wide-eyed at lions, tigers and bears. There was also a variety of aquariums, each with different kinds of fish and other undersea creatures. In one tank, a young woman was hand-feeding fish.

They went around the zoo until they were tired and hungry and stopped for a delicious meal and a little rest and relaxation.

Finally, the sun was beginning to set, so they got back into the motorhome and went to the place they had parked before.

They popped some popcorn and laid back to watch TV. "Where are we going next?" Nancy asked.

Gavin thought about it for a few minutes and then said, "How about Eisenhower Tunnel? I wonder what it's like to drive right through a mountain and then maybe we could go to Pikes Peak."

"Sounds like a good idea." Casey said. "There are several lakes down that way and we could go for a boat ride and do a little fishing. Then, it would be time to head home for graduation. We can go down through Gunnison and down to the flat lands. We can stay at one of the motor parks and, by the middle of tomorrow, we should be home. Do you want to go to the apartment or the Bed and Breakfast so we can show off all the pictures we took?'

"Let's go to the Bed and Breakfast." Gavin said. "We can show everything we did, and we could probably spend the night and go to the apartment in the morning so I can get some of my exercises done."

The evening was spent ooh and wowing over the photos. "Josh, we've got to take a trip like that someday. Those pictures are incredible. Who is this family? 'Chelsea said.

"They're family that has a concert band and believe me, they are good, Chase said. They said if they were ever doing a concert where we were, we should come and they gave us some free tickets."

Chelsea studied the photo and said, "There's going to be a concert Wednesday night after we lockdown and we were planning to go. This picture looks just like them."

Casey took the picture and studied it. "You're right. It is them. Do you want to go, Gavin?"

'You bet! I'd like to see them again. I like good music."

Chelsea took a count and it looked like everyone intended to go.

Wednesday, they locked up and everyone piled into their cars and they head for the park, where the concert was being held. They were setting up the folding chairs when they heard someone say. "Well, look who's here!" Casey turned around and gave a big grin. "Ralph." he said, "where's the rest of the family?"

"They're inside getting things ready. Hey, Honey!" he yelled. "Come on out. The guys we met at the parking areas are here and they brought some other folks." Mable brought the kids out and introduced them. "Ralph plays guitar, I play violin, Jackson plays Banjo and Sandy plays trombone and Jimmy just plays. I see he's having a good time playing with your dog.'" They all laughed, and Casey started introducing his bunch. "This tall guy is Josh and the pretty lady beside him is his wife, Chelsea. Next to her is Maud and her new hubby Stan. The young guy is Bo, he's Chelsea's brother. He has a pack of sled dogs. He's having Rusty, his lead dog trained as a search dog and his second is Bella; He's having her trained for search and rescue. Maud owns the Bed and Breakfast. That last guy is my best friend, Gavin." "You should come over after the concert and relax and spend the night. If it's okay with you, I'll take Jimmy down to the pens and introduce him to my dogs." Bo said Jimmy started jumping up and down. "Can we go see the dogs, Daddy? Please, pretty please?"

Ralph thought about it and looked at Mable. She looked down at Jimmy and nodded. "He'd love it and it would feel good to be in a real house. We like our motorhome, but sometimes. I'd just like a night in a real house with a real bed."

Ralph dug into his pocket and handed them all free tickets. "We'd better get over there and get started." They got out their instruments and the concert began. Their music was incredible and between every song, the crowd whistled and applauded.

The concert lasted about three hours and, when it ended. The crowd praised them and slapped them on the back. "Hope you come back soon." Someone shouted.

Casey and Josh helped them get everything loaded and led them to the Bed and Breakfast.

"Oh, this is a very nice place. Mable said.

Maud said, "I hope you like hot ham and cheese sandwiches, iced tea or coffee and Ice cream, which you can have chocolate syrup or strawberries with whipped cream on it."

They all made their choices and waited somewhat impatiently for their order. Jimmy gobbled his down and licked his lips. "Dat was weel good! he exclaimed. Now. can we go see the dogs?"

Bo took Jimmy down to the kennels and the child down to the kennels. Jimmy was jumping up and down with excitement. "I wike dem. They weal pwetty. I wish I could have dem all!."

"If your parents say, it's alright. It's still light and the dogs and I'll I'll take you for a ride on my sled. We can go out in the field and ride around. Let's go upstairs and see if it's okay, Bo said.

Bo explained what he wanted and Jimmy's parents were happy to see their son so excited. Bo started to take Jimmy downstairs again but noticed the two older boys seemed disappointed. He grinned at them and said, "Would you two like to go with us?"

They looked at each other and then, grinning from ear to ear, rushed to join the fun. Downstairs, they helped Bo get out the sled and watched while he attached the wheels he used in the summertime. Then, he took it out and hitched up the dogs. "Everybody ready, he asked." They nodded and looked as if they were going to be a given a fortune. "Okay." Bo said. Oldest first and strap in. Then, next oldest and finally, Jimmy. "Is everyone strapped in?" They all nodded. "Good. I've already got the dogs hitched up, so we'll start slow and then speed up." He took them around the field and then speeded up a little. His dogs obeyed every command. Ralph and Mable watched as Bo took the boy in circles and short strips, larger circles and the full length of the field and back, with more circles. For an hour, they went up and back and forth and around and around. Finally, Bo stopped, got everyone unstrapped and then took the dogs back to their kennels. "Well, boys did you enjoy your ride? I take people for trips in the snow and, sometimes. I take people for two-day winter camping trips."

Chattering and laughing, the boys climbed the steps and went inside. Ralph shook his head and smiled. "Those kids had so much fun. I wished I was as young as they are," he said.

Bo laughed and then said, "If you have a concert this way next winter, come on over and I'll treat the whole gang to a two-day, winter camping trip. I think you'd all get a kick out of that."

Ralph laughed and said. "Sounds like fun. We'll think about it and let you know. I guess it's time for us to head out. We have a concert tomorrow and we need to get ready for it. Being here has been a pleasure and we thank you for welcoming us."

Everyone stood on the front porch and waved goodbye. "They're nice people." Maud said."I do hope they come back. Sometime."

"I guess it's time we were headed home, too." Casey said. "I've got to get ready for graduation and then my team will be sending someone to get me started training. Just thinking about baseball gets me excited."

"While he's training, I'll take care of Buddy and I'll have a new therapist. He thinks he can help me make good progress." Gavin said.

Casey grinned and said, "When you get to walking properly, are you finally going to propose to Nancy? She's going to get tired of waiting pretty soon."

"Don't you worry. The therapist says I'm doing real good and taking care of Buddy while you're training will give me even more exercise. When are you going to meet a real nice woman and pop the question?"

"Don't you worry," Casey said. 'There are a couple of gals at the university I've had my eye on."

"When will you start playing?" Gavin asked.

"When the season starts. They'll probably put me in as a starter for two or three weeks, so they can see how I do. If they approve of me, I'll be on full-time. I can hardly wait." Just then Buddy came out of the bedroom, jumped on Casey and began smothering him with slobbery doggy kisses. "Hey there," Casey said, "it looks like Gavin has been taking good care of you. How about I go in the kitchen and make some supper? Will Nancy be here tonight?'

"No, she has a training class going; she might be here later." Gavin answered. 'She's getting more and more business. People are getting more dogs to protect their homes, businesses and children. When she gets here, she's worn out.

"Then, I guess I'll make enough spaghetti in case she comes late. I'll make some salad, too and I think we have enough ice cream for dessert."

They ate a hearty supper and then sat back and watched television. One of their favorite programs was on for them to enjoy.

When Casey was at the University getting ready for graduation, Gavin took care of Buddy. His legs were getting much, so he used his crutches and went down the elevator and out to the fenced animal play yard. He took a rubber ball for

Buddy to fetch and laughed at the happy-go-lucky as he played in the yard. When Buddy got tired of playing, Gavin cleaned up any mess the dog had made, and they went backups to the apartment. Then, Buddy would stretch out beside Gavin and take a nap. When Casey came home, Buddy would jump up and run to him to give him a good tongue slurping.

Nancy came over two or three times a week with a pizza and a firm kiss for Gavin. She was happy that he was making so much more improvement. She gave Casey a peck on the cheek and they ate their pizza. Then, she began teaching Buddy. "He's doing wonderfully." She said. "Gavin has been taking good care of him and he learns quickly. He's a spectacular dog." She sat down beside Gavin and he put his arm around her. He turned her face toward him and said, "Nancy, I have something important to ask you." He took a deep breath and said, "Nancy, I'm in love with you, but I didn't want to say anything until I was mending. But now it's time. Will you please marry me?"

Her mouth gapped open and tears ran down her cheeks. She wrapped her arms around his neck. "Oh, Gavin, I've been waiting so long to hear you say that. I was afraid you didn't want to be with me forever. Yes! My darling. I will marry you whenever you want."

He wiped the tears from her cheeks and said, "I was afraid you wouldn't want to marry a cripple. Then, Casey kept urging me to work harder at it and taking care of Buddy has given me the push I needed to do my best. I love you so much I don't know what I would do without you. I can walk good enough to go up the aisle to the most beautiful woman in the world. Decide when it's good for you and I'll be ready."

The minute I get home, I'll start planning, she said. "Casey will be the bridegroom and Buddy can be the ring bearer."

"We have one more person we need to tell about our getting married," Gavin said.

"Who's that?" Nancy asked.

Gavin grinned and said, "Mr. Chang said if we ever got married, he would make us a wonderful meal and a beautiful wedding cake. He's such a nice man. When Casey, and I, go there, he always brings us an extra treat. And he always asks about the beautiful young lady who gets our favorite pizza to bring home to me. We couldn't leave him out of the event."

"He could be the escort for the bridesmaids. I think he would look great in a tuxedo." Nancy said.

When he brought out their food, he asked when the wedding would be. Gavin thought a minute and said, "Well, Casey graduates next week and then, he'll be in baseball training for two or three weeks before he turns pro. He won't start playing until the season starts but he'll still be practicing.

He wants to be his absolute best, so he works hard at it. I'm really proud of him."

Nancy said, "I have an appointment at a Bridal Shop to try on some gowns, but I'm afraid I'll pick out the wrong thing for me. I'm nervous as a caged cat."

They all laughed and Mr. Chang said, "You beauty young lady. No need you be nervous. Everyone sees you in wedding dress, and they think you beautiful."

Nancy asked, "Do you have a tuxedo? We'd like you to be the escort for the Bridesmaids."

"You want me in wedding? I have tuxedo. When wife, and I get married, I wore tuxedo. I keep for special occasions. I be happy to be in wedding party. Be sure to tell me when it be so can get food and beautiful cake ready for it. I so happy for you."

Nancy stood up, put her arms around his neck and gave him a kiss on the cheek. "We'll be so happy to have you join us. I'll send all the information as soon as everything is settled."

Full of excitement, they headed back to the apartment. Nancy and Gavin were happy that Mr. Chang was going to be in their wedding party. With Casey graduating and going into training, it would be a few weeks, but that would get her gown and get the arrangements made. Her mother was as excited as she was.

The next weekend, Nancy and her Mother and friends, met at the bridal shop so she could try on dresses. They spent the afternoon with her trying on dress after dress until she finally settled on a pale cream-colored dress with long sleeves trimmed in lace. The train was long and lavishly trimmed with and the neckline covered her throat with lace. The ladies all oohed and awed at how beautiful it looked on her. The veil was a cap with beautiful lavishly embroidery and a train that went just below her knees.

Later that day, she and her Mother went to the church to talk to the Pastor and make the wedding arrangements. They didn't know the exact date, but Nancy scheduled it between Casey's graduation and when he would start playing with the Yankees.

Nancy was so anxious, if it weren't for training dogs, she would have been a nervous wreck. Her business was growing and planning for the wedding was wearing her out. She would go to Gavin's apartment, cuddle against his shoulder and take a nap. He smiled as she nestled against him. When Casey came in, he would shush him so he wouldn't wake her.

Casey would go into the kitchen and heat some soup and sandwiches for when Nancy woke up. When they had finished eating, the rest of the evening was spent just relaxing. As it got late, Casey would take Buddy to the fenced backyard, so he could do his business. After Casey cleaned it up, they went back to the apartment and headed for bed. Casey crawled under the covers and Buddy stretched out beside the bed. It wasn't unusual for Casey to wake up and find Buddy cuddled up beside him. With a smile, he would smile and rub Buddy's head and scratch behind his ears. Buddy would give him a couple of slurpy kisses and then snuggle a little closer.

A couple of weeks later, Casey came running in with a newspaper in his hands. "Look here!" he said excitedly. "There's an announcement about your wedding in the paper. It doesn't give a date. It just says it will be before Yankee season starts, and details will be announced later!"

Chapter 22

Unfortunately, they were unaware that two other men were also reading the newspaper. "Look at this." Bull said. "There's going to be a wedding and it told who's going to be in it. One of them is the guy we're after. It tells where it's going to be, and I think we should we should check out the location. If there's a good cover, we might be able to get our guy. Let's check it out and then get back to the house and do some planning.

"Okay, here's what we'll do. We'll take a stroll along the sidewalk across from the church to see what kind of cover there might be. If there aren't any trees or bushes, I know there'll be cars parked along there for the wedding guests. We can hide behind one of them."

"What if more people come?" Snake asked. "They might see us."

"We'll dress real nice, and I'll wrap up a box to look like a wedding present. If anyone else shows up, they'll just think we're there for the wedding. They won't pay any attention to us."

Snake chuckled. "Bull, you're a real smart guy. You always know just what to do."

Bull patted him on the shoulder. "You're pretty smart too, my little friend. When we get back to the farm, I have another plan."

"How are we gonna know when the wedding will be?" Snake asked. "It didn't say in the paper."

Bull grinned. "All we have to do is read the daily paper. This last issue said it would be before the Yankees get ready to start playing, so we'll know when to get ready. The paper, before the Yankees start, will probably tell when the wedding is going to be. I can hardly wait. In the morning, we'll take a walk by the church, and then, we'll go buy some nice clothes so people will think we're guests."

As they pulled into the garage, they saw their boss sitting on the porch, having a snooze. The creak of the gate woke him and he yawned and said, "I wondered where you boys had gotten to."

"We took a ride around the countryside." Bull said. "It's sure getting pretty. The trees are all leafed out and flowers are blooming everywhere. I like this time of year. How would you like hot ham and cheese sandwiches and potato salad for supper? We could finish it with some of that ice cream you bought the other day."

The old man grinned and said, "That sounds right good to me. You know, you're a real good cook."

Bull and Snake went inside and started making supper. Snake boiled potatoes and chopped onion for the salad. With supper ready, Bull called the old man.

They got the dishes done and went into the living room to watch TV for a while. The Sports channel announced that the Yankees would have their starting game in two weeks. "That sounds good," Bull said. "I like the Yankees. I'd like to take some time off to see the game."

The Old Man smiled and said, "If you want to see the game, help yourselves. You can take the pickup. I'm going to be visiting my daughters, and the kids, for a while. You can take care of the place while I'm gone. There's plenty of food in the freezer, so you won't get hungry. I'm not sure when I'll be back. I'm gonna hit the hay, and I'll leave in the morning; after I get my bags out to the car."

"Are your bags ready?" Snake asked. "We can load them for you tonight if they are. Then you can have time for breakfast before you go."

"They're packed, but I don't want you to have to carry them out. You're probably tired."

Bull slapped him on the back and laughed. "We're happy to help you. We've had a great place to live and plenty to eat. It's a lot better than it used to be. Sometimes we had to go hungry before we could collect enough to buy a hamburger. You take it easy on your trip and have a good time." He went into the man's bedroom, picked up the suitcases, carried them to the car, and put them in the trunk. "There, he said, now you're all ready to go. Snake and I are going to my bedroom and playing checkers. You get a good rest, and we'll see you in the morning."

As they watched the car disappear down the road, Bull and Snake started dancing a jig. They would have the place to themselves for a week or two. That gave them plenty of time to plan their act of murder. Driving the old pickup and dressed like a pair of hillbillies, most people ignored them. They even talked like they were from the hills. They met an elderly walking along the sidewalk. "Howdy, Ma'am. Shore is a purty day, aint it! Bull said. "Indeed it is, she answered, the sun is shining and the flowers look so beautiful. Are you folks from around here? "No, we got us a place up in the hills but we had to come down for some food stuff. Nice to meet you, take care."

As they walked down the sidewalk, Bull slapped Snake on the shoulder and said, "See, I told you nobody would know us. Let's go down to that store where they sell paper. I have an idea that can get us paid. I'll tell you about it when we get back to the house."

Bull bought a roll of news 'print paper, and the clerk asked if he was planning to start printing newspapers. "No. Bull said. "We have a bunch of kids coming over, and I'm going to show them how my Dad used to print. We're going to pretend to print a paper. They'll put their stories in it. One of them will make up a story about flying saucers and draw pictures about them and aliens. They're all my two sisters kids and we're taking care of the six of them tonight. I know we're going to have a lot of fun. I have a computer and printer, so I'll print their paper and they can take it home. My buddy and I will keep the copies. I'll frame the prints and hang them on the wall. Kids have such incredible images and I can't wait to see what they all come up with. If I get time, I'll bring the copies in and show you how clever they are."

"That sounds like it could be fun," the clerk said. "I have nephews that are always making up stories. Some of them are pretty good. I may try to get them to print a newspaper. Your idea is a good one.."

"You're right. Getting kids to use their imagination does them a lot of good."

Bull gave the clerk a wave and went out the door. Snake said, "It took a long time just to get some paper. Snake said.

Bull grinned and gave him a story about what he had told the clerk that would keep him from wondering why he had bought the paper.

Snake slapped his hands together and said, "Man, you are a clever dude."

Dude laughed and began singing an old cowboy song, "I'm an old cowhand from the Rio Grande."

You know how smart those cow hands were when they were driving cattle all over the country. Well, that's how I feel. I've got something at the house I'll show you. I'll put it on the front of my newspaper and send it to the Boss."

Bull showed Snake a picture he had cut out of the paper when Josh was getting married. I thought it might come in handy, and it will. When I was younger, I worked in a place where they printed newspapers. I learned how to do newsprint. The old man has a computer and printer, so I'll do a page and send it to Makil.."

Snake gestured somewhat frantically and said. "But we don't know where he is! He hasn't kept in touch with us for quite a while!"

"Don't worry. I know a lot of people who can find out where he is and let me know how to get in touch with him. I'll let him know where to meet us. We'll get paid, or he'll wish we had. We've gone through too much for him to try and play games with us. Just in case he tries anything, I'll be armed and he won't get away with it. I'm kind of hoping he tries something because I don't like that man. I think he'd try to cheat us. Since he hasn't been keeping in touch, I'm thinking he's going to try and something rotten."

Bull went into the computer and started working. Snake paced and fidgeted. He wasn't sure Bull's idea would work, but he was willing to go along with it. Bull came in to get a glass of wine and saw Snake pacing around. "Take it easy." he said. "It'll take a while to hear from him and we'll have everything ready just in case he tries anything." He went back to the computer and got busy again. When he came back into the room, he said, "I'm getting hungry, so I think I'll fix us something to eat."

Having the old man gone for a while is going to make things easier on us. I think we'll go down to those rocks in disguise. I'll let my beard grow and wear bib overalls, a checkered shirt and scruffy looking boots. I'll use some makeup, so my face looks old. We can dress you up so you look about ten years old. I'll get you a toy gun and you can pretend you're shooting at stuff. If anyone sees you, they'll think you're playing, and you can pretend you're hunting injuns. If there are kids around, they'll want to join you. I'll watch to see if the guy we're after is anywhere around and after a little while, you can say 'Daddy, I'm hungry' and we can go get something to eat. Then, we'll go to a hamburger stand and get something to eat.

When they got back to the house, Bull went into the office and got everything set up so he could print his phony newspaper. He got himself a cup of coffee and a couple of cookies to nibble on and then got busy. A few minutes later, he came stomping out, an angry look on his face.

"What's wrong." Snake asked.

"That old computer is giving me fits! I'm going to try to get it to work right. If I can't, I may have to get another one. I know the perfect place where I can get a good used one a used at a cheap price. He put on some shabby clothes, got one of the old canes the Old Man used, jumped in the pickup and took off. When he got to a small secondhand computer store, he hobbled in and looked at the computers. When he found one he liked, he went to the young man at the counter. "My old computer gave out on me and I like that one, but I can't carry it." The young man smiled at him and took it to the counter. "Does it work? Bull asked. "It's almost new. The man that owned it passed away and his family didn't want to keep it, so they brought it to me." Bull stroked the computer and said, "I need a printer, too but I can't afford both of them, so I'll just take the computer." The clerk smiled and said, "You remind me of my Dad, so I'll let you have the printer free."

Bull hung his head and pretended to wipe tears from his eyes. "You are a generous young man and I thank you so much. I like to keep in touch with my grandkids, but my hands give out on me. How are you going to get it into your house?" "I have a little table with wheels. I can slide it off and push it up the ramp and in the door." "Bless you for being so kind." He gave the clerk a hug and showed him to the truck. They got things loaded and secured. As Bull left, they waved at each other. The young man stood there and shook his head. "Poor old fella. Probably lives alone and uses the computer to keep in touch with other people."

Bull glanced through the back window and burst into laughter at the way he had bamboozled the clerk. He liked it when he could cheat someone. When he returned to the ranch house, he hollered for Snake to carry things in. When he told Snake what he had done, they both laughed until their bellies hurt.

"I'll get started in the morning. It may take at least a week because I want it to look real. When Makil sees it, he'll believe we've done our job, but we have to find a place where he can meet us. We don't want anyone to be suspicious."

"What about the first place we used as hideout?" Snake asked. "There's a lot of trees and brush where we could hide the pickup."

Bull thought for a minute and said, "That's a good idea. There's no one who lives nearby. I think we should go check it out. Let's go out there right now and see what condition it's in."

"Before I get started on the newspaper, let's go and check the place out. When Makil sees it. He'll think we're making sure nobody spots us and wonders what we're doing after we look the place over. We'll head back to the farm and I'll get the newspaper going. As soon as we know where he is, I'll send the paper and when he's ready to meet us, we'll head to the hideout."

Bull worked on his newspaper for over a week and. then showed it Snake. "Wow." Snake said. "this looks like the real thing. I just wonder how long we'll have to wait before we hear from Makil. "

It was another week and a half before they got a phone call. It was Makil. "Okay, boys, where do we meet? I'm glad I got the paper and we can finish this business. I'm sorry I couldn't get back to you a little sooner, but I've been in China doing some important business. I don't know your territory, so you'll have to guide me in,"

Bull gave Snake a thumbs up. "Just head toward town and we'll meet you at the highway. We'll be in a pickup truck. Just stay behind us and we'll lead you to a hideout where there isn't anyone around who might get nosy."

They were beginning to think Makil wasn't going to show when an expensive car drove up and Makil stepped out. He walked over and gave Bull a slap on the back. "Nice to see you boys again. Looks like you did a good job. Now, where do we go?"

Bull and Snake climbed back in the pickup, turned on the country road and headed back to their hideout. Makil followed close behind them. When they got there, they pulled into the brush and trees and Snake got out and told Makil to pull in with them so they couldn't see the vehicles if someone drove by. Then, they all went inside. Makil looked around and said, "This is a great place to meet. No one would suspect there was anyone here. Now, we need to get into business." He turned, with his back to them and laid his briefcase on a table. "I guess you'd like to get paid." He took some bills out and waved them over his shoulder. "See these bills? There's more in this case. Just give me a minute to get out what I've got here." His arms moved and he counted. But, when he turned around, he had a pistol in his hand. He pulled the trigger and Snake tumbled to the floor. He didn't realize that Bull also had a gun. When he turned, two shots rang out. One hit Makil in the chest, the other between his eyes. He crumpled to the floor and Bull walked over to him. "I never trusted you!" he said as he smiled down at the dead man and then took the money from the briefcase.

They didn't know that a man, who lived down the hill, was walking his dog and heard the shots, but he thought someone was hunting. When he had almost reached the top of the hill, he saw two men come out of the old house. The short man seemed to be hurt and a large man was helping him. He saw them get into a pickup that was hidden in the trees and take off. He walked over to the house and looked inside. There was a man lying on the floor, in a pool of blood. He took his phone out of his pocket and called the police. He was standing outside the door when the patrol car came.

"I'm Officer Jack Carter. I need your name and to know what's going on?" The Officer said.

"I'm Andrew Brady. I live just down the hill and I was walking my dog when I heard shots. I saw two men come out of the house, get in a pickup that was back in the trees, and take off. I went over to the house and saw a bloody man on the floor. I went in to check on him and saw he was dead. That's when I called you"

The Officer went in the house and then came out to radio the in the homicide. It wasn't long before another Patrol car and an ambulance arrived. "What's going on, Jack?" the second Officer Bob Simms, asked.

"A murder. Mr. Brady went to the house and saw the body. That's when he called us. He was walking his dog when he heard the shots. He saw two men come out of the house. They got into a pickup that was hidden in the trees. Then, they took off. One was short and the other was tall and husky. They were headed toward town and probably passed you as you were on the way out here." They slipped on rubber gloves, went into the house to put the body in a bag, and then carried it to the ambulance. When the ambulance had gone, Jack told Mr. Brady he would have to go to headquarters and look at some pictures.

"Ok, but I'll have to take my dog home and put him inside. Then, I'll have to leave a note for my wife. She's in town and will wonder where I am. Then, I'll be right down,"

Jack smiled at him and said, "Take as much time as you need. We're open twenty-four hours a day."

The officers watched him leave and then went back in the house to look for fingerprints.

They went back inside and looked around "Holly Cow! There are fingerprints all over the place." Jack exclaimed. "Look at this!" Bob said. "It's a briefcase. It's full of papers and bullets. I'd say he came, loaded for bear." Making sure his gloves didn't smudge anything, he closed and locked it.

"Be right back," Bob said. "I'll get what we need for the prints out of the car." He brought in a jar of fingerprint dust, a soft bristle brush and a roll of clear tape. Bob put the dust on any prints he saw. Brushed it carefully over the prints, which turned them black. Then he put a strip of clear tape over them. Jack had found a frame with clear, unbroken glass in it. He made sure it was clean, so Bob could put the clear tape with the prints on it. "You know," Jack said. "The description Mr. Brady gave me sounds like those two guys that were shooting at the Bed and Breakfast. Let's get back to the station and see if Mr. Brady is there, yet." Bob carefully laid the frame in the back seat. Then, they got in their vehicles and headed for town. Just as they parked, Mr. Brady walked in the door. Bob got the frame out and followed him in, "Follow us and we'll show you where you need to go to review the pictures." Jack opened the door. "Cody," he said, "this is Mr. Brady. He's here to look at some pictures to see if he can identify some possible killers. Take your time. If you need anything, Cody will take care of you. We have to go and try to get some fingerprints identified. They went to the lab and handed the frame to the technician. They're from a possible murder. While you're working, we're going to get something to eat and a cup of coffee. It had been a long day, so they sat down comfortably and put their feet up. Just one more hour and they could go home and relax. Jack wanted to hold his little daughter and Bob wanted to hold and kiss the woman he had recently parried. Sometimes it seemed as if the day would never end.

They were both so tired, they dozed off. Then, they heard a voice. They woke and blinked. It was the Chief. 'His hands were on his hips and a grin on his face. "Working too hard. Boys?" Jack groaned and said "I think I'm always working too hard." "Well. This time you did a good job. The prints are from two hired killers, wanted in six states for murder" and Mr. Brady identified the pictures. "It's Monte Makil, head of the gang the other two worked for. We have one dead and are searching for the other two."

Chapter 23

After killing Makil, Bull looked around to be sure they had left no incriminating evidence around.

Then he went over to check on Snake and found he was still alive. "Come on, Buddy. Let's get you in the truck and head for the house so I can get you patched up. He got you in your armpit. I'm going to rip down one of the curtains and make a pad I want you to hold in place real hard."

When he got the pad in place, he helped Snake up and got him settled in the pickup. "Hold it tight, we'll soon be at the farm."

Unaware that they had been seen leaving from the old house, Bull pulled out of hiding and sped toward the farmhouse. He pulled into the garage, got Snake out and into the house, and laid him on his bed. "I'm going to get that bullet out." He said. "Then, I'll bandage you up and keep an eye on you. I don't think the slug is very deep." He went and got a pair of pliers and bandaging. He took Snake's shirt off and could see the bullet wasn't very deep. Snake yelled as Bull pried for the bullet and yanked it out. He put a pad over the wound and wrapped him in bandages. "There, a little rest and you'll be fine. I'll fix us something to eat and bring you a plate. You just rest easy."

Bull went into the kitchen and fixed some ham and cheese sandwiches and coffee. He carried it into the bedroom, propped Snake with some pillows and put the plate on his lap and the coffee on the nightstand. "You eat and I'll get you something for the pain,"

Bull got himself something to eat and went back into Snake's bedroom. "Well, you're eating and you don't look too bad. The pain pill must be working. I'll turn on the TV and we can watch a movie." He watched for a while and saw Snake was asleep. He turned off the TV, pulled a blanket up around Snake's shoulders and went outside to check on the livestock.

The next morning, he put Snake's arm in a sling and got him into the kitchen, where he had made scrambled eggs, toast, and coffee. "You look like you're feeling pretty good. I'm going to show you what we got."

Snake's eyes got big as Bull counted out the money he had taken from Makil's briefcase. It was far more than they would have been paid.

In a couple of days, with his arm in a sling, Snake felt good enough to go outside and feed the chickens. He didn't like dealing with livestock, but he loved feeding the chickens. Bull shook his head and asked, "Why do you always want to feed the chickens?" "Because, when I was a kid, I always fed them. When they saw me coming, they would run to me and if I sat on the ground, they would pile up in my lap and cluck and peck at my fingers. They were my best friends. I hated it when my Dad would butcher a couple for Mom to cook. I felt like I was losing a friend. I never ate any of them. I just ate whatever Mom had cooked. If I was messing around with them, instead of doing some other kind of work, my Dad would slap me and tell me to get to work. When I was twelve, I took my favorite hen and ran away from home. They never did find me. Henrietta and I lived in cardboard boxes until she wandered into the road and got hit by a car. I cried and buried her and even made a little cross for her grave." Bull patted him on the back and said, "I know how you felt. My Dad was always drunk and if I didn't do what he wanted. He'd slap me around and lock me in the closet. One time. He forgot and I was in that closet for three days. I was fifteen when I left home and joined a gang. We holed up in the basement of an old garage. We stole the food we ate, beat up people and took what they had. That's when I met Makil. I never did trust him, but I did what he told me to do and I got paid for it. Then, I met you and got you into the business. The first time I shot someone, I was real scared. I figured the cops would get me. You probably felt the same way when you shot someone and got paid for doing it."

"Yeah, I was scared, but I got used to it and I liked getting paid. I didn't even mind it when we had to hide out for a while." They started in the house to fix lunch when they heard a car pull in. They turned to look and saw it was the old man they worked for. He was back sooner than they thought he would be.

He came back carrying a pitchfork. He aimed it at them and said, "I want you off my property right now. Get your stuff and bikes and get gone."

Bull slipped his hands into his pockets and asked, "Is anything wrong? We've worked real good, for you. Why do you want us to leave?"

The old man glared at them and said. I stopped to put gas in the car and saw two wanted posters with your faces on them and it said you were wanted for murder. If you don't want this pitchfork in your guts, you'd better get your stuff and those motorcycles and get off this land."

Bull gave him a nasty little smile and said, 'When we go, I suppose you'll call the cops."

"I'll give you five minutes to be gone."

Bull pulled his hand out of his pocket and grinned as the old man dropped to the ground. Then, the dog attacked and tore a hole in his pants. He kicked it and then shot at it. "We need to get our stuff and get out of here," Bull said.

"Are we taking the bikes? "Snake asked.

"No. We're taking the delivery truck you painted and wrote the logo on. Anyone who sees it will think it's to deliver stuff in. It was a good idea for you to disguise it."

They hurried to gather everything they had and loaded it in the truck. Then they backed out and hurried toward the highway. "It's a good thing you shot the old guy. He could have called the cops and told them where we were heading." Snake said.

They didn't know that Bull had barely nicked the old guy and he was playing dead. He took his phone from his pocket and called the police. In minutes, they were there. He told them what had happened, what they would be driving and the direction they went.

The Officer sent out the information to the highway patrol and they laughed. The way they were heading, there was no crossroad. They would have to turn left or right because they was being blocked from both directions. If they tried to turn and go back, that would also be blocked too. They had gotten themselves into a trap they didn't know about. An ambulance took the old fellow to the hospital and one of the Officer that knew his dog picked it up and took it to the vet.

When Bull and Snake reached the highway, they saw there was no crossroad. They turned left but had only traveled about five miles, when they saw that the highway was blocked by patrol cars and officers were waiting, with weapons drawn.

Bull did a quick turn around and they headed the other way. They hadn't gone far when they saw patrol cars blocking the highway and more officers waiting with weapons ready. "Get out the side door and start running across that field. Bull said. "They may try to chase us, but we have guns to hold them off with. If we can get back to the house, we can get the bikes and they won't be able to catch up with us."

They climbed out of the truck but had to crawl under a wire fence. They started running, but the Officers leaped the fence and gave chase. Bull and Snake turned and shot at them, but trying to run and shoot at the same time kept them from hitting anyone.

Snake began to tire from his bullet wound and he fell to the ground. A couple of Officers handcuffed him and took him back to one of the patrol cars. They kept an eye on him while the others were still chasing Bull.

Bull stopped and fired several shots and hit an Officer in the leg. One of the Officers handed him a handkerchief. "Here," he said, "wrap this good and tight around your leg and call an ambulance. We'll need one for you and the perp." Then he took off, with the others to catch Bull.

Bull didn't know he was running toward a river that was deep and flowed fast. He turned to fire a shot, but his foot slipped on the sloping bank, and he tumbled into the fast-moving water. He didn't know how to swim and thrashed around and screamed, "Help! Help! I can't swim." The Officers ran along the bank, trying to keep ahead of him before he could drown. When they were far enough ahead, one kicked off his shoes and dived into the water. Bull was sinking fast until the Officer grabbed his collar and lifted him from the water. Then, the others waded in and helped drag Bull up onto the river bank. They turned him on his belly and cuffed him. Then they pumped and saw the water gush from his mouth. He began to sputter as water flooded out of him.

They got him to his feet and walked him, stumbling, to a Patrol car and strapped him in. Then, all the Patrol cars headed into town where the criminals could be treated for their injuries and then taken to the jail to be locked up.

One of the local officers went into Dan's room and said, "The Patrol caught the guys that shot you. They're locked up right now. I hear you're going to get home in a few days; your dog is at the vet, doing fine. When you go home, one of us will bring him out to you and we'll keep an eye on you to be sure you're okay." He patted Dan on the shoulder and said, "You take care of yourself." Then, with a wave, he left. "Those are good boys," Dan muttered. "They always want to help someone."

When Bull and Snake had healed, they were cuffed and taken to the courthouse. Their papers were handed to the judge and when he had finished reading them, he frowned at the two men. "When the jury hears about you two, you aren't going to be real happy about their decision."

Bull leaped to his feet and shouted at the judge. "There isn't anything to go bad for us. I know a real good lawyer and he's got lots of people. We'll walk out of this place, free as birds. You can count on it!"

The officer behind him pushed him back in his seat. "Keep your dirty hands off me," Bull shouted.

"I have a case I'm working on now." The Judge said. "But I'll schedule this trial for three weeks from now."

The Officers took Bull and Snake, screaming and cursing back to the squad car. When they had them locked up in their cells again, Bull stomped around his cell. Screaming and swearing and pounding the walls. Snake grabbed the bars and said "Why don't you just shut up? All that noise won't help a thing."

Bull walked over to the bars and punched Snake hard in the gut. Snake stumbled back to his cot and moaned. "You know what the jury is going to say." He groaned, "we just don't know what the judge is going to say, and all your noise won't help."

Bull sat down on his cot. "I'm going to call that lawyer. He'll get us out of this. They can't deny us a lawyer. "

He yelled for one of the Officers and said, " I want to call my lawyer " Jake came over, took the number and handed Bull the phone through the bars. "Let me know when you're through." Bull listened for an answer, but there was no answer. He hung up and dialed another number. This time, he got an answer. "Hello, came a man's voice, 'Jerry, this is Bull. Where's Kelly? He isn't answering." "Kelly is dead." Jerry answered. He was drunk and stepped in front of a truck." "You're his partner and I need a lawyer." Jerry laughed and said, "I wouldn't be your lawyer for a million bucks; you're nothing but a jerk. I'm surprised Kelly wasn't kicked out of being a lawyer."

With a shocked look on his face, Bull dropped the receiver through the bars and sat down on his cot. His elbows were on his knees and his face was in his hands. "Something wrong?" Snake asked

"My lawyer got drunk and was hit by a truck. He's the only lawyer I've ever used and he always got me free when I got in trouble. He could have gotten us out of this seem we're in. I don't know anyone else as good." In three weeks, we go to court, but I don't know anyone here who would stick up for us."

Three weeks later, they were taken to court. They had little to no chance.

The Judge came in the courtroom and action began. The charges were read and the jurors were led to a private room to make their decision. In less than an hour, they came out.

"What is your decision?" The judge asked.

The leader of the jurors lifted the paper and said, "We find these men guilty of murder and attempted murder and recommend the most serious punishment."

The judge banged his gavel and said, "The court sentences these two men to life imprisonment without parole."

Court is dismissed.

ABOUT THE AUTHOR

My name is Pat Rogers. I'm eighty years old but have always had a passion for books. I wake up at night with a new book, poem, or song running through my head. I don't know how to write the music, but I know how the songs sound. I have so many handwritten books that I decided it was time to start getting them published. This is my third. I hope you enjoy all the people and activities in this book. I'd love to hear from my readers. Just go to patrogersbooks.com.

www.ingramcontent.com/pod-product-compliance
Lightning Source LLC
LaVergne TN
LVHW040150080526
838202LV00042B/3104